The Most Perilous Sideshow

A Sophie Mae Adventure

Mason Bell

For Lucas, Oliver, and Jacqueline

THE MOST PERILOUS SIDESHOW

A SOPHIE MAE ADVENTURE

MASON BELL

A PLEASANT SPRING BREEZE CARRIED THE EARTHY FRAGRANCE of rosemary across the field of the Gardenia Estate. The yellow and blue triangles of homemade banners waved from the tops of wooden posts and gave the picnic area a festive feel. Today was Sophie Mae's 18th birthday, and excitement filled the air.

Off-key singing of "Happy Birthday" grew louder as Mrs. Worthington led the family, holding a two-layer cake with pink icing. Sophie Mae smiled and raised her hands to her cheeks. She'd known about the party, but it surprised her they even bothered to care about such minor things with the world still burning.

The Great Depression raged on despite it being 1937, nearly ten years since the stock market crash sent the dominoes of the economy into freefall. People across the country struggled for food and shelter, both of which were in short supply. But on the estate, life was green and lush, and boredom was the biggest enemy.

Three heart-shaped candles towered over the cake, and Sophie Mae gathered her breath. *I wish for...* her thoughts trailed off. What would she wish for? She had a warm bed and plenty of food, not to mention a family that doubled as her friends. Maybe for the return of her memories stolen by the traveling box, to put her and the family's minds at ease? Though they had good intentions, their endless stories of life on the Drycrop farm grew old and were as foreign to her as living on the moon.

Closing her eyes, her chin stretched toward the cake. The tiny fire of the candles waved under her slight breath. Suddenly, her head jerked to the side as the young boy saved from the train station tugged on her pant leg. "Let me. Please, Miss Sophie."

"All right, James." Sophie Mae lifted the six-year-old boy to the cake.

Taking in a deep breath, he held it for nearly an entire minute, most likely making a wish himself. A light shade of blue started at his cheeks and spread to his eyelids. Sophie Mae patted him on the back, and a gust of exhausted, lung-stored air burst from his lips.

As he gasped for air, Billy gave him a thumbs up from the other side of the cake. "Good job, little man! That's some evenly placed spit for an amateur."

"All right, gentlemen," Mrs. Worthington said. "Now,

fetch the plates and forks, please."

Dink angled for her brother, slugging Billy in the arm. A bright smile covered her face as she hustled to Sophie Mae. "Can you believe you're finally an adult? What should we do to celebrate—after all this, of course?"

"Let's go to the lake. Billy says there's a new floating island for jumping."

George the Great hurried toward Sophie Mae and threw his arm around her, passing a finely wrapped gift with the other hand. "This is for you. It's from Oscar."

"Thank you." Wrapped in periwinkle paper, the gift encompassed the whole of Sophie Mae's hands as she placed it on the glass table. The ribbons puddled graciously as she tugged them off. The lid fit so tightly it produced a fart sound as she wrenched it off. Her warm cheeks blushed as Billy and James chuckled behind her.

Removing a layer of delicate white paper revealed a set of hair combs with vibrant blue and red jewels set in a diamond pattern along the edge—a folded card lay beside it with Oscar D's perfect handwriting.

Dear Miss Sophie,

I wish I could be there for your big day, but this gift will have to do. I hope you like the color of the jewels. My grandson Nathan helped me pick them out. He has a much better eye for this sort of thing.

I'll be home before autumn arrives to help with the planting. We can dig in the dirt and catch up.

With love,

Oscar D Mayville

"Those are quite lovely," Aunt Catherine said. "I haven't seen a matching set since I was a child. They're very rare."

"Oh, get on with it! Cut the cake!" Billy screamed.

"Get on with it!" James copied, his hands resting on his hips.

"James, mind your manners!" Betsy said.

Judy struggled from Betsy's grip as she followed her older brother James, who ran for the safety of the barn. The small family of three moved from the train station to the estate two years ago after Sophie Mae offered the Mayville cottage to them.

Betsy looked to George with exhaustion in her eyes. "What am I gonna do with that kid?"

"He'll be fine. All boys are a little wild at that age."

Dink smirked. "But Billy never grew out of it."

"Now kids, today is Sophie Mae's day, and we'll not have any fighting. Who wants the first piece?" Mrs. Worthington held out a plate with a slice of cake. With a sinister laugh, Billy raced by and grabbed the treat, vanishing into the barn.

Sophie Mae held two plates while perfectly sliced pieces were placed on their surfaces. She spotted Mr. Langston and Ms. Ruby sitting in the cool shade of the oak tree. A smile grew across her face as they laughed and carried on.

"Cake?"

"Thank you, Miss Sophie," Mr. Langston said, taking a plate.

Ms. Ruby patted the cushion next to her. "Won't you have a seat? You shouldn't work so hard on your own birthday."

Sophie Mae sat close and rested her head on the woman's

shoulder. Since Aunt Catherine's return to the estate two years ago, Ms. Ruby had become a softer, less aggressive role model for everyone.

"You're growing so fast," Ms. Ruby said, brushing Sophie Mae's cheek. "I hate to see it. One day you'll leave us, and then what will we do?"

"You always say that. Where would I go? Everything I need is right here in Evenland."

BURRUP!

Sophie Mae covered her ears at the broken trumpeting coming from behind the red barn. All eyes shot to Gus Grizzly, who marched and danced toward them blowing on a trombone. Whispers between the residents grew as they tried to guess the tune that had no rhythm or style. Sophie Mae gave no thought to the song's formality and clapped as best she could with the music. *He's so funny—what a show.*

Mary Louise strutted from behind the barn wearing a feathery hat and matching purple cape in spectacular circus fashion. Her trunk curled tight as she high-stepped to the music, marching after Gus.

Leggy brought up the rear, holding a basket in her teeth. Not one to don a silly costume, she wore a simple polka-dot bow tie at the base of her neck.

George the Great jumped from his seat and joined the parade, raising and lowering his arm like a drum major in a marching band. The troupe moved into formation, and George outstretched his arms. "Without further ado, The Miss Sophie Mae Spectacular!" Bowing, he dashed to the crowd and sat with Betsy and Judy on a plaid blanket.

Gus Grizzly threw his toy trombone to the soft grass directly in front of James and Judy. They looked at each other, and their eyes grew wide. James scurried across the grass like a lizard while Judy hopped to her feet and ran, each wanting the instrument. Holding it high like a trophy, Judy touched it to her lips and continued the marching tune.

Swooping passed Leggy, Gus grabbed the basket and shot to the sky, stopping mid-air and tipping it for the audience to inspect. The basket flipped upright, and Gus reached inside. Grunting and tugging his arm from the opening, he revealed a red ball.

Below him, Mary Louise and Leggy swayed side to side with the music, watching the sky for their part. As Gus released the red ball, it looped and dipped as it hurtled to the ground. Mary Louise stepped a few feet to the right and grabbed the ball from the air with her trunk.

Gus reached in again, but this time produced an orange ball. Rolling it from his fingertips over his shoulders to the other hand, he lobbed it.

Leggy galloped back and forth, following the arc of the ball. Confident of its landing spot, she hoisted to her back legs and grabbed the ball with her teeth. Strutting to Mary Louise, she nervously loosened her bite, allowing the ball to balance perfectly atop the red.

A final ball fell from the sky, moving faster than the rest, as if it hid a tiny rocket at its core. Leggy shot to her hind legs, and her eyes followed its spiral descent. With her front hooves, she caught the speeding prop and balanced it on top of the other two, making the tip of Mary Louise's trunk resemble a triple-decker ice cream cone.

Much like a cannon, Mary Louise propelled the balls into the air with the top blue ball darting across the field. Leggy caught it between her horns and rolled it along her neck.

Bouncing off her bristly tail, it landed in James's waiting hands.

The orange ball shot even farther, just past the rose garden. An audible gasp came from the residents as it zoomed over their heads toward the angel statue erected as a memorial for Myrt. The ball flew to the marble carving and dropped into the angel's outstretched hand like the outfielder of a baseball team.

Mary Louise and Leggy danced in a circle and kicked their legs outward as the red ball hung suspended over their heads. Gus clapped, and the ball drifted like a leaf in autumn, landing perfectly on Mary Louise's trunk. Strutting and flapping her ears, she curtsied to the audience and rolled it toward Sophie Mae's feet.

Gus Grizzly clapped once again, captivating the audience with anticipation. Music, like that from a jewelry box, grew louder as the mysterious red ball tapped Sophie Mae's shoes. Before she could grab it, the ball shot high into the air, drawing all eyes to the red streak it left in its wake.

BOOM!

As the ball exploded, a shower of pastel confetti rained on the spectators. Cheers and whistles encouraged Mary Louise and Leggy to take a bow. Gus Grizzly flew overhead, dropping wrapped taffy from the Thomas Candy Shop. Green polka-dotted parachutes carried the sweet treats to the opened hands of the kids.

"We wish you the happiest birthday, my dear," Mary Louise said as Sophie Mae cuddled her trunk.

THE LATE-MODEL TWO-DOOR SEDAN SPED ALONG THE QUIET highway. Brunhold rested his arm on the opened window, enjoying the cool morning air. An orange light blinked next to the fuel gauge, showing he'd have to stop at the next fuel station. In a hurry to find his long-lost wife, stopping to refuel was a delay he didn't have time for.

His wife, Betsy, wasn't actually lost but tucked away in a train station in a small town called Evenland. Brunhold found her more difficult after learning a second child was on the way, resisting his pressure to steal the growth formula from her ailing father.

Brunhold had dumped her at the depot that was once

heralded as a majestic feat of engineering. The depression had transformed it into a dump, a common sight across the country as people lost their jobs and ruin overtook public places. A sinister grin spread across his face, forming dimples in his cheeks. *The weakness of the American people is on full display. I hope they have seen this back home.*

A sign with a red star and green 'T' hung in the sky about half a mile down the desolate road.

Texaco
Full Service

The stiff pedal resisted the force of his foot, but a swift kick had the car speeding down the road, shortening the distance between the fuel station and his car.

His front tires swerved under the cement archway, triggering the bell inside the shop. A young man in a white uniform glanced out the window and set his soda on the counter. Stepping from the booth, he waved to Brunhold. "What can I get you, sir?"

"Ten gallons, leaded."

"Right away, sir."

As the youth hurried to fill the tank, Brunhold leaned to the glove box for the paper map. Unfolding the first section, he followed the green travel route he'd marked a day prior. *One, maybe two hours out. I'm making good time.*

Finished with the refueling, the youth knocked on the sedan's window. "$1.70, sir."

Brunhold passed two whole dollars through the window. The gas station attendant waved enthusiastically at the large tip as Brunhold pulled from the station.

. . .

BY MID-DAY, Brunhold's stomach growled, pleading for him to stop once again. Passing into the city limits of Evenland, he scanned the frontage roads for a place to stop and eat. A plain square building sat next to a tall metal pole that held a busted sign. It served as a warning for weary travelers to wait for the next stop. But Brunhold knew of worse places back home. The car jostled along the cracked drive as he parked in front of the entrance.

The inside of the restaurant was no restaurant at all. Cots lay head to foot along the floor with only minimal space between them. The stench of armpits and old fryer grease cured his hunger.

A ragged woman with a kid on her hip entered the main room, her eyes fixated on a piece of paper. Judging by the deep squint of her eyes, it was a bill with a large balance. Her bare feet shuffled along the dingy tile. "Hudson, look at this —" She grabbed the child tighter at Brunhold's harsh expression.

"I'm assuming the restaurant is closed?" Brunhold asked.

"Ain't no one got money for food. We sell shelter now. 10 cents a day. No pets."

Brunhold grinned at the woman's suggestion he pay to sleep in a crowded room on a flea-ridden cot, but a quick glance revealed several desperate people had taken the woman up on her offer. Returning to his car, he resolved to drive straight to the train station and forgo food.

As the car parked at the train station, he winced at the awful state of the area. A Hooverville had grown in front, and the breeze carried the odor of rotten eggs. He rolled up his car windows and locked the door before heading to the stairs of the station.

Protecting his hand with a handkerchief, he pushed through the rotating glass door and scanned the waiting area. Benches remained mostly empty, and trash congregated in the corners collecting loose hair and dead bugs. The natural light pouring in from the domed ceiling was its only redeeming quality. *Serves them right for the harm they brought to my country.*

Prowling the walls and hidden corners of the building, he found no sign of Betsy. He'd expected as much, having left her there years ago. Brunhold crossed the floor to the restrooms, strutting into the ladies' room without hesitation. Empty.

Brunhold brushed his lapel and checked his hair in the ladies' room mirror. Strutting out of the heavily tiled room, he walked to the ticket counter. Recalling the frail man who worked behind the desk, Brunhold accepted the risk he might be remembered. The general population didn't take too kindly to men who ditched their families because of hardship.

"How may I help you, sir?"

"I'm searching for my sister and her children," Brunhold lied. "They fled our family home when the droughts began. I've crossed the country, and I believe they're here, possibly living in the station. Have you seen them?" He slid a picture of Betsy and the kids to the man.

Setting his glasses on the tip of his nose, the ticket clerk pored over the photo. "I've worked in the station for the last two decades, and I've seen many people. I remember this family, but they've been gone for years. Might have moved into the Hooverville. It's not much better, but she could've."

"Thank you. If you see them, could you please call? It would mean a lot to my family and me." Brunhold handed him a card with a phone number printed in black ink.

"Will do."

STEPPING through the makeshift gate of the Hooverville made Brunhold angry. Mostly because it smelled of garbage, but also because it reminded him of the motherland.

Since the Great War, many innocent Germans had suffered under the debt placed on them as reparations to cover civilian damage of other countries. Families lost their homes, and the children born under the oppression had a bleak outlook for the future.

Finding Betsy in a more cooperative state was the answer to the country's food shortage problems. Her dad, Benjamin Miller, was a world-renowned botanist and on the cusp of a rapid-growth formula for crops. With him having lost his mind, Betsy was Brunhold's next best hope.

Meandering through the narrow sidewalks of the Hooverville, he spotted an older woman carrying a basket of stiff, line-dried clothes. When she took notice of his watchful eye, she dropped the load. Her feet pounded against the packed dirt as she fled to her doorway and hurried inside.

Brunhold plodded over the unfamiliar path and knocked on the wall of her hovel. No answer. "Ma'am, I'm looking for my sister. Could you help me?"

The woman peeked from behind the moth-eaten curtain that posed as a door. Brunhold wanted to ram the woman into the home and take the information he needed, but he knew patience would win the day.

"I can't help you none," she said.

"She is about this tall with brown hair. She has two small kids with her, a toddler and a baby." Having to mention those kids made his insides burn with anger. More than an inconvenience, they drew Betsy's attention from his mission. "Here's their picture."

The woman glanced at the image before turning her steely gaze to the man. "Like I said, I can't help."

"I'd be willing to pay you."

A tall man with a thick beard approached Brunhold. He dropped a bag of black coal to the dirt. "The lady said no. Now, I don't know what it means where you come from, but here it means get lost."

Brunhold clenched his fist at the man's disrespectful tone. Instead of attacking, he stumbled from the hovel to the outer wall of the Hooverville. *I need something to barter. Food, medicine. Money has no value here.*

Passing back through the gate and overgrown weeds, a pale, thin kid in need of a doctor tugged his elbow. "Sir, I know the family. I used to play with the boy, James."

James? That's what she named the oldest offspring. Such a foolish religious name for a kid.

"Can you tell me where they are?"

"How much were you gonna pay Mrs. Baker?"

Brunhold grinned at the cleverness of the boy. Opening his wallet, he flicked a crisp five-dollar bill. "About this much."

The boy's yellowed eyes stared at the money as he spoke. "She left the village before my 8th birthday two years ago. My momma says the woman in the big house saved her, and now James's mom eats all day and has lots of warm blankets."

"Which house?"

"The one in town with the gardens and the magician." Brunhold flinched at a car backfiring in the parking lot, and the kid snatched the bill from his hand and disappeared between two hovels.

The big house with the garden? What is the kid talking about?

Following the trail of the boy, he needed more information.

One by one, the family members excused themselves from the birthday bash as the sun set over the estate. Betsy ran across the field and snatched up Judy, who didn't want the fun to end. Kissing the girl's cheek, she recalled the dirt once layering her skin when the small family lived in the train station.

Judy's wiggling and screeching caught the attention of George the Great, who removed his top hat and dropped it to Judy's head where it fell to her nose. "If you and James take a bath, you can keep my hat."

"Forehter?" Judy asked with a big grin.

"Yes, forever. What do you say?"

The three-year-old held her finger to her lips, and her eyes darted from George to Betsy. Clutching the hat tight to her head, she raced to the cottage, catching up with her brother James and tugging his shirt. "Please take a bath. Please, please, please."

"Cute kiddos," George said. "They have grown so much over the past two years. Why, Judy was just a baby when you moved into the cottage."

"Sophie Mae saved us." Betsy turned away. "If it had been left to me, they might not have survived this long. What was I thinking trying to live in a train station? I'm such an idiot."

"You did what you thought was best. You gave Judy and James the best shot at getting food, and the station kept them dry." George pulled her close. "Besides, if you hadn't stayed there, Sophie Mae wouldn't have found you. We might have never met."

Before losing herself in the warmth of his arms, she remembered the cottage was temporary, and she could be homeless in an instant. The guilt returned. *What was I supposed to do? He left me with no money. Those kids are my life...*

"Look, it worked like magic!" George said, pointing to the top hat bobbing across the threshold of the small home, once occupied by Oscar D and his late wife, Myrt.

"I'll make sure you get your hat back," Betsy said, winking. "What's a circus magician without a hat?"

"Let her keep it. I've been considering some new clothes after having these forever. They're wearing thin."

"But, you're George the Great," Judy said. "You love the circus. Besides, how will I even recognize you without those long tailcoats."

"I'll see you tomorrow?"

"Not until the evening. I have to work in the morning. We're reducing the price of some items to help the community. Money is so tight, people are buying the expired food and picking off the moldy bits."

Betsy dropped his hand as she turned for the cottage and the promise of resting her feet. *If he knew the truth about me, he wouldn't be so generous with his compliments. Agh! Does he have to be so nice*?

Inside the cottage, she wedged the sweaty sandals from her blistered feet. She closed her eyes for a few seconds and rubbed her hair as the sour expression on her face was replaced by a faint smile. "Here I come, you little monkey children!" Betsy meandered to the bathroom, grabbing toys along the way.

Screams and laughter rang through the house as the kids raced to their usual hiding spots. Judy peeked from under the pile of dirty clothes while James, being slightly more creative, slid behind the floral print curtain covering the sink's pipes. His dirt-packed toenails stuck out from the ruffle along the bottom.

"You can't hide from me. I can smell the mud and bugs clinging to you." Betsy marched around the small room, checking random cabinets and drawers, encouraging their imagination by saying 'not here' after each failed attempt.

Betsy recoiled at the coldness of the porcelain tub as she leaned inside and twisted the knob. Warm water flowed into the deep basin. Tiny feet pattered across the tiled floor, ending with Judy splashing into the tub and soaking the walls of the small room. "I got you, Mommy!"

After half an hour of scrubbing, a brown ring of dirt clung

to the sides of the tub. Betsy hurried the freshly cleaned kids to the bedroom where they climbed into the bed. Like toy soldiers at Christmas, they slapped their arms to their legs. Betsy fluffed the blanket a few times before dragging it to their chins, tucking it under their backs and legs until they were sealed into the bed.

"Now I'm a mummy, just like you," James said.

Betsy leaned over the bed, netting the full attention of the kids. She stroked their hair as she sang a lullaby her father taught her as a child.

Rosewood oil soothes the soul,
Striking at the dark.
Argon seeds heal the mind
Imagination from olive bark.
Snake tooth ground fine
Offers hope to the land.
Can the magic of the future
Stop the ever-blowing sand?

With a kiss on each of their foreheads, she left the room. Folded blankets from the coffee table drifted in the air as she spread them across the cushions of the couch. The cottage had one bedroom, and it was important for the kids to have a comfortable bed. Being uncomfortable had become a way of life since she'd met Brunhold.

She closed her eyes and focused on the chirping of frogs in the garden outside the window, hoping to fall asleep before the irrational thoughts returned.

Betsy turned on her side and clutched the blanket to her eyes. Brunhold's face often haunted her thoughts, and tonight was no exception. *How could you dream of saving others while your own family wasted away in a train depot?*

Moonlight shone through the cottage window, and she flipped to the back cushion of the couch, focusing on what she needed to do, not on what she wanted.

WITH HIS ARMS FREE OF THE LAB COAT, GEORGE TOSSED IT TO the rack, missing the hook by three feet. Panic struck as he glanced at his watch for the second time in ten minutes. He dashed up the laboratory stairs two steps at a time. Being late had become his calling card since taking on the task of finding a cure for Ernest's shrinkage.

Bursting through the not-so-secret kitchen door, he darted up the grand staircase to the second floor. His anxiety made the trek down the hallway seem longer than usual. George caught his breath as he stopped at the door and brushed his hair flat. He knocked.

"Come in," garbled a voice from inside the room.

In all his years at the estate, George had never ventured into the sewing room. Walking through the doorway, his eyes darted from one brightly colored fabric to the next. Spools of thread lay in a special shelf along the back wall next to baskets stuffed with trim and tassels. Like the lab, the room had a sense of purpose.

"Right on time," Mrs. Worthington said, crouched at the waist of a sewing dummy. "I was working on a new pattern. Times are changing. Pants are becoming the fashion for women, and men want more comfort from their clothes."

George weaved through the tables and stacks of magazines featuring finely dressed models. "Don't let me stop you. I have time now."

"Nonsense." She tucked away the pincushion. Grabbing a few pieces of paper from the desk, she sat on the coffee table across from George. "I sketched a few ideas for your new pants and shirts. The lighter fabrics will give you more flexibility for working in the laboratory." Mrs. Worthington struggled to highlight the finer details of the cut. Learning to read upside down wasn't a side effect of the potion.

"If you don't mind?" she motioned to the seat next to him on the couch.

"Certainly."

Moving next to him, Mrs. Worthington ran her fingers across the sketch's hemlines and darts. George nodded and tapped his temple, but he'd no idea what she was talking about. The stiff fabric of the magician outfits served him well in most climates and extreme weather events.

"What do you think?" she asked.

"I think it'll be great. Is that all you need from me?"

The sketch dropped to her lap as she examined his expression. "Have you ever been fitted for clothes?"

"Not that I remember. In the circus, you get the hand-me-downs from the last guy. Thankfully for me, he was my size, and I didn't gain any weight. The costume designers were usually preoccupied with the trapeze swingers and clowns. Those were the real messy jobs where the costumes took a beating."

"But wouldn't the lights and heat make the clothes fade or tear?"

"Yeah, but who's gonna notice when I'm in the center ring pulling live chickens from a local woman's frilly hat?"

"You have a point. Come with me." Mrs. Worthington led him to a three-way mirror with a cubed wooden stool. "Stand here while I measure you."

George waved his arms, admiring his reflection that seemed wider at the head and longer in the legs. "You've had funhouse mirrors all this time?"

"Hardly. But if I did, I'd get one that made me look taller."

Twisting toward her, he realized she wasn't as tall as he thought, but why hadn't he noticed before today? Squinting one eye, he took a guess. "Five foot two?"

"Something like that. It's not really important. Now stand still before I poke you with a pin. Arms out."

George lifted his arms. Mrs. Worthington held a pencil securely in her teeth as she stretched the floppy tape from his hip to his ankle. After a quick note on a pad of paper, she measured from his shoulder to his wrist.

The small white hairs of his neck stood as she measured

the width of his neckline. *She smells amazing, like wildflowers in a field. Why haven't I noticed this before?*

"Do you wear perfume?" George asked, cringing at the awkwardness of the question as it escaped his lips. "I meant… I was thinking of creating a fresh scent to sell at the general store. You could be my tester?"

"I'd love to. Do I receive free bottles for life?"

"Yes, assuming it smells good, of course."

George locked his knees, vowing not to say another word. Picking up a new project wasn't his idea of fun. Plus, he didn't know the first thing about making perfume. *Maybe she'll forget. I can use Ernest as an excuse. It's the truth, after all.*

With the measurements jotted into her notebook, she patted George on the shoulder. "You can drop your arms now. We're done."

"Thank you, for…the…" his jaw dropped as he stared past her head.

"What is it?" she said, concerned.

"Duck!"

A barn owl with large hunting pupils shot from the far end of the workroom. Mrs. Worthington screamed and covered her hair against the creature swooping and pecking at her barrettes. George grabbed her by the shoulder, and they scurried under the waist-high cutting table, watching the bird land on a spool of blue tassel trim. It gave them the stink eye before pecking at its wings.

"Billy," Mrs. Worthington fumed, making a note in her memory pad with bold lettering. "That boy will be the death of me."

"Or the life of the party when he gets older." George

smiled. "It's difficult to catch an owl with their swiveling heads. Why is it in your sewing room?"

"If I knew these things, I wouldn't be hiding under a table."

"I have a plan. If we crawl to the door with our heads low, it's unlikely he'll see us as a threat. It worked when I was a kid, and a robin chased me a mile from my house for stealing its egg."

"Do you know a lot about animals?"

"Not really. Unless we're talking elephants, then, yes, I'm an expert."

"I guess anything is worth a try at this point."

George popped his head from the table and glanced to the bird, whose head bobbed along the downy feathers inside its wing. "Now."

Mrs. Worthington clutched the skirt of her dress near the hem and crawled after George. Looking back with fear, the owl seemed unconcerned with their grand plans for a clean escape.

Slower than snails across hot cement, they inched to the door. George reached for the glass handle as Mrs. Worthington screamed. "Hurry!"

The door flung open, and they darted to the hallway, cowering along the paneled wall. George cradled her shoulders as she protected her hair with her hands. Dipping from the doorway, the owl bumped into walls and knocked paintings to the floor. The laughter of young boys perked George's ears. "I hear a couple of pranksters."

Mrs. Worthington released her skirt and fluffed the pleats as she followed George to the banister, spotting Billy's and James's heads protruding through the railings. Their eyes chased the owl as it swirled and dipped in the foyer's open space in search of an open window.

Sneaking up behind the occupied jokesters, George lifted them by their collars. "Boys, get that owl out of the house."

"How am I going to catch it?" Billy asked. "It's so fast."

"Like you did the first time, I suspect."

Billy waved to James. "Come on, let's get the net."

James skipped to the stairs and each step to the first floor. "Are we gonna catch it again, Billy? Can I use the net this time?"

Mrs. Worthington and George watched for owl droppings as they followed the boys to the dining room. Her distraught eyes met his. "Ms. Ruby will not like this."

Billy jumped to the crisp, white table cloth of the dinner table, kicking over flower vases and breaking long, tapered candles in half.

Soaring higher to the tall ceiling, the owl smirked, smug in its ability to escape the hunting party. Billy floated up from the furniture, swinging the net at the bird.

James crawled to the dinner table and stomped over the flowers, grinding their red and yellow petals into the fibers of the table cloth. Each time the bird swooped low to evade Billy, James swung a napkin using it like a net.

"I suggest we get going before Ms. Ruby sees this mess," George said. "I should get back to the lab, anyway. So much to do."

"Your work needs you. How's Ernest holding up?"

"Well, he's short on time…"

"Stop it!" she said, holding his arm. "I have plenty of sewing to keep me busy as well. Excuse me."

George leaned on the banister as she moved gracefully up

the stairs to the second floor. In all his travels with the circus, he'd never met a woman with such a generous heart. Most mothers yanked at their kids' ears and swatted them for speaking out of turn.

Stepping over the tipped plants and toppled chairs of the dining room, he strutted through the kitchen to the basement lab. *It wouldn't be too hard to make perfume. If I could make it smell like her, I'd be rich.*

GEORGE THE GREAT BURST INTO THE LAB AND GRABBED HIS lab coat, interrupting the dust drifts exposed by the rays of sun. Scratching at a clump of dried jam on the lapel, he knocked on the door of the dollhouse. "Rise and shine."

With disheveled hair, a four-inch-tall Ernest emerged from the doorway of the dollhouse wearing a blue-and-red tracksuit, a contribution from an Olympic doll clothes set. George placed his hand near Ernest's feet, but his offer for a lift was ignored.

Ernest stepped from the half bookcase and climbed down the rope attached to the shelf. From the cobblestone bricks to the leg of the sturdy work desk in the musty room, he used the rope ladder he'd installed last year to get to the surface. Like taking the stairs, he climbed the spines of several stacked books and took a seat eye level with George.

"I've brought you a gift." George took a tiny suit from his pocket and laid it next to Ernest. "Mrs. Worthington made this for you. It'll be better than those doll clothes you've been wearing. Now you can be yourself instead of a chef or a scuba diver."

Ernest barely glanced at the new clothing.

George straddled the stool at the work desk, resting his elbow on the desk and his cheek on the palm of his hand. "I know the potion to fix your size isn't going to plan, but you understand it takes time."

Ernest's eyes remained focused on the cement flooring. "How could I have been so naïve? I let my greed and anger move me to a place of violence, and now I'm the size of a toad living in a girl's dollhouse."

"It was the potion. You had no choice," George stood and paced. "I should've never given anyone the potion. It needed more testing."

"That might be, but I was angry long before the potion. Remember those days back in the circus? I hated the owner—Spenwaller. He was an outstanding example of the men whose greed ruined this country."

"Well, that was a long time ago, friend. This suit is a chance for a new beginning. A fresh outlook. Why don't you try on the jacket? What could it hurt?"

Ernest lifted the suit from the toothpick hanger, examining the stitching and buttons on the front. His arms slid through the openings and the sleeves of the jacket landed right at his wrist. A perfect fit.

George leaned on the counter as Ernest tested the buttons and flicked the collar to cover his neck, delighted in his interest. *There's nothing like a new suit to give a man purpose. There's no end to Mrs. Worthington's cleverness.*

"It fits like my normal jacket, maybe better."

"Good," George said. "She'll have your lab coat ready for the afternoon. You can help me with the potion, like old times, without the drama."

Ernest crawled behind the stack of books and reappeared wearing the suit. He finger-brushed his hair into shape and smiled at George. "Yes, without the drama, George the Great."

"Just call me George."

"Only George? Does this have anything to do with Betsy? I've noticed the two of you spending more time together. James tells me you gave your top hat to his sister."

George placed a ladder on the cabinet and grabbed the basket of cleaned vials from the top shelf. "Betsy or not, it's the right time to move on from my past. Sophie Mae has done so, and she seems fine."

"Sophie didn't have a choice. The traveling box stole her memories, so she doesn't struggle with her past. That's the hard part." Ernest strolled around a beaker and scratched a water spot from the glass. "You don't suppose I could borrow a traveling box and wipe my slate clean?"

"Not a chance. You'll be better off by confronting the past. Besides, I destroyed the boxes and shelved the potion for good. There's no room for sloppy magic."

"This entire lab is sloppy. Books are half on the shelf and half on the floor, not to mention the chemicals are spread out on each counter. A man of science would never leave his lab in such disarray."

"Should we start today's work by organizing the potion cabinet? We could make a run into town for supplies we need for your growth potion. I thought a little wormwood might work. Maybe a bottle of wild magnesium drops."

"Those ingredients do encourage growth in plants, but first we need to organize. You're the big man around here. Why don't you clean, and I'll read over the notes and make a shopping list?"

George dropped a pile of cotton cloths next to the books. "Good idea, since you're the one whose been keeping notes for the last year. I can't read my penmanship, much less your little scribbles. The words look like a splattering of ink dots, without a magnifying glass."

Several notebooks were moved to the desk, and George took the red-covered one and placed it open on the surface. Ernest clutched the edge and turned the page as he plodded across the notebook, reading and taking notes for their supplies trip.

"Thanks for helping me out," George said. "We really do make a great team."

"Are you kidding me? I tried to tell you that a decade ago."

"Maybe you taking a quick trip in the box isn't such a bad idea," George said, twirling his mustache. "Then, with half your memories erased, I'd be two steps ahead of your quick wit."

"You'd need more than a mind erasing box, giant."

DINK TRUDGED THE STAIRS TO THE THIRD FLOOR AS SOPHIE Mae gave her a gentle push from behind. Charity meetings with Aunt Catherine, the estate owner, usually happened in the kitchen and were more boring than helping her mom darn socks. Today, the missus wanted to meet in the imagination room.

"Why are we talking about charity stuff there?" Dink worried. "The place should be reserved for fun. This feels like a trick. A rotten adult trick."

"Maybe she has something special to show us?" Sophie Mae added.

"I doubt it." Dink stopped at the door entrance and tied up her shoulder-length hair.

Sophie Mae worried. Dink had lived in the estate longer and might know better. Twisting the glass handle to the imagination room found it dark and eerily quiet.

Dink peeked around her shoulder. "I told you so. This won't end well."

"The room is in either a memory or a thought. See, the buildings are growing solid."

"It's got to be a memory," Dink said. "Everything looks ancient."

"How can it be a memory? Everything's in black and white, even you. I'm pretty sure the earth has been in color from the beginning."

"Told you. Trick." Billy's prized baseball bat appeared in Dink's left hand as she stepped warily along the sandy path.

"Welcome to The Circus!" Aunt Catherine said, stepping from behind a tent. "Pretty amazing, yes?"

Sweat dotted Dink's brow as she pointed to a horse charging toward them. "Not good!"

"Don't worry. He's not after us. Watch."

No sooner than she'd spoken, a man in a bowler hat and baggy pants hobbled past them, twirling a cane and speeding up as the horse galloped closer. He didn't acknowledge them, as if they were invisible. Sophie Mae watched as the awkward man turned the corner and disappeared, the horse charging close behind.

Aunt Catherine patted their shoulders. "Don't you know the movie? *The Circus*? Charlie Chaplin?"

"Oh, yeah," Dink said. "That was ages ago. I've seen the

poster but not the film. Dad was sick when it was in the movie house."

Sophie Mae moved closer to Aunt Catherine. "We're in a movie?"

"Yes, dear. I do it all the time." Aunt Catherine took her hand, leading them to the Big Top where a broken banner decorated the scene. A group of disgruntled clowns mumbled and trudged out of the scene behind an angry man in a top hat.

"Was that Georgie?" Dink asked, craning her neck for a better look.

"No. What a shame you haven't seen this movie." Aunt Catherine sat down on a round cable spool and crossed her legs. "That was the end of the scene when the ringmaster, who isn't George, tells the clowns they aren't funny. At least now we have the place to ourselves for our meeting. Well, until the next scene in this space happens."

Sophie Mae sat next to Aunt Catherine. "I brought the food supply logs for the Hooverville. The government's new programs are helping people earn more money, but everyone is saying food is more scarce than last year."

"And, Dink?" Catherine asked. "Did you bring the soup kitchen numbers?"

"Yes." Dink blindly handed over the papers, keeping her eyes on the clowns that jumped and rolled in the sandy ring. Her face wrinkled with regret. "Why did we meet here again? And why are there so many clowns?"

"That's part of the news," Catherine said. "I've seen improvements in earnings as you have. An old friend from Hollywood wants me to be part of a charity drive to collect money for whatever the city of Evenland needs. Several of the actors working in this movie are volunteering to help the cause. I thought you might like to see them in action."

Suddenly, the ringmaster reappeared and posed between Sophie Mae and Dink, deep in thought as the clowns bumbled around the ring. A large man raced into the tight space. His words to the ringmaster seemed hostile but silent as the grave.

"Why can't I hear him?" Dink asked.

"It's a silent movie, dear."

"No sound. How is that entertaining?"

Sophie Mae ignored Dink's question. "How can we help with raising money? Will we have parties on the estate? Do we need to set up the guest rooms?"

"That's the hard part. I'll be leaving tomorrow morning. The dinners and live performances will be in California. There's a good pocket of wealthy people there."

Dink, oblivious to the conversation, pointed to the actor flopping along a spinning platform. "Why is that man's face so white? Surely, he doesn't look deathly ill in real life."

Aunt Catherine furrowed her brow. "You're a very sheltered kid, Dink."

"That's what I keep telling Mom!"

Sophie Mae grew irritated. "The actors have on makeup, so you see their faces better, and if you watch their lips, you can tell what they're saying. This movie is ten years old."

"Only ten? How's that possible?"

"Can't they do without you in California?" Sophie Mae asked, returning to Catherine. "With both you and Oscar D gone, who's gonna make sure we stay on track with the charity?"

"You will, dear." Aunt Catherine sauntered to a traveling wagon with yellow panels and an extravagant red arch across the top. A full-grown male lion slept behind the bars of the cage. His thick mane ruffled as she approached.

"You trust me with this?" Sophie Mae asked. "It's crucial to the community."

Catherine pet the mane of the lion, and it purred, licking her arm. "You'll manage just fine. I'll go west and find money to house our friends in the Hooverville. Two sides of the same coin."

"Can we go now?" Dink asked as a young lady with a pale complexion wearing a tutu danced past, sashaying to the silence.

"That's all I have for you," Aunt Catherine said. "Stop the film!"

Ticking of the film reel slowed to a stop, and the black-and-white scenery faded into the paneled walls of the imagination room. Dink bolted for the hallway. Sophie Mae and Aunt Catherine meandered behind her.

"That was awful. I'll stick to the real circus."

Aunt Catherine hugged Dink. "Tonight, Mr. Kimall is coming over for dinner. We'll discuss the trip in more detail. I hope you'll recover by then, Miss Dink."

Heading to her room across the hallway, Aunt Catherine waved to Sophie Mae. "Don't worry too much. You're going to do fine."

Dink burst to the first floor, flinging herself from the banister to the dining room and out the doors to the fresh garden air. Standing on the paved patio, she outstretched her arms. "Ah, that's more like it."

"I can't believe she's leaving us," Sophie Mae said, as she joined Dink on the patio.

"Who's leaving?"

"Aunt Catherine…she's going to California."

"Why?"

"Didn't you hear anything she said? She's going to raise money for Evenland."

"Oh, that's why we entered the creepy movie. It was a Hollywood show and Hollywood's in California."

"You're a mess, Dink. A real mess."

"Thank you!"

FROGS CROAKED AND BIRDS STIRRED UNDER THE DARKNESS OF the early morning. Henry Langston pulled on his white dress shirt, pressing the buttons through the buttonholes. One sock, then another, led him to his dress pants.

It's nearly time for the 8:00 a.m. wheat delivery. He walked to the closet admiring the neatly aligned, identical pairs of shoes—all of which were missing their laces.

He knelt to the row and picked up the first and last shoe, searching for the laces underneath the soles. No luck. Henry strode from the room in his socks, his heels pounding on the hard floor. His feet ached with each step as he wasn't one to walk without shoes.

Holding the handrail as he descended the stairs seemed the best way not to slip and fall to the first floor. Plodding to the kitchen, he flipped on the lights and opened a few drawers, finding forks, knives, and hand towels. He stopped at the clicking of heels.

Ms. Ruby's uniform comprised a tight-laced pair of ankle-height boots that clicked louder than all other heels worn in the house. Crossing into the dining room, the clicking grew faint, but never slowed. Ruby never dawdled when she worked, a quality Henry adored.

"Ruby?"

The basket of dirty clothes pushed against the swinging door, and the odorous stench announced her entry into the kitchen. Grabbing the last towel and tossing it into her basket, she turned to the butler standing in his socks.

"Are you feeling quite alright? Where are your shoes?"

"My shoes are exactly where they belong. It is the laces I am having trouble locating. Have you seen them?"

"Why would I know where your laces are?" Her eyes squinted into tiny slits. "But I think I might know who does. Billy wasn't at dinner last night. If that ain't guilty, then I can't tell the future. Follow me to the laundry room. I might have a spare set or two."

Ruby and Henry crossed the kitchen to the laundry room. Through the archway on the back wall, she switched on the lights growing from dim to full brightness. "If Billy is teaching James everything he knows, we could be in trouble for the next fifteen years."

"It's not so bad. I used to cause a little trouble myself at that age."

Her lips pursed as she gave a wayward glance. "You? In

trouble?" Moving forward into the laundry room, she tripped. Towels and socks jumped from the basket and rained down as she struggled to her feet. "I don't know what's come over me? How did I fall?"

Henry helped her stand, then searched the doorway for signs of Billy.

"I found my laces." Henry knelt to the black shoestrings tied in knots end to end. They stretched across the doorway, a danger for those not expecting such a thing. "It looks like a tripwire, but nothing tripped."

"Except for me," Ruby said.

CRASH!

A crate, one taken from the barn, flipped from the top shelf and tumbled to the tiled floor. Both of them looked upward, worried about what clever prank the boys had concocted and what fate might befall them.

All at once, gray and white chicken feathers drifted from the wooden box and shrouded the room. Feathers ranging from the long outer wings to the downy fluff near the body caught the breeze flowing from the opened window. The quickness with which they scattered about the place impressed Henry.

"What is happening?" Ruby yelled.

"Cover your mouth against the feathers. It will be over soon."

The breezy spring day kept the feathers circulating around the room, allowing them to land on surfaces high and low. Ruby put her hands to her hips and glanced over the washing machine and ironing board covered in the mite-ridden feathers. A small blurt of a giggle sent her hand covering her mouth. Another escaped her lips and became a hearty laugh.

Henry plucked a feather from her hair and tickled her nose, laughing at the strange start to the day. "It's like being in a bird blizzard."

"What is wrong with those boys?" she said, smiling. "It'll take half a day to tidy up these feathers."

"Not if we allow the boys to clean up their own mess."

"Good luck finding them. They have more hiding spaces than a cricket in a lizard cage."

Ruby set the laundry basket on the ironing board and tossed the loose socks inside. Reaching for one behind the washing machine, she staggered backward at the screeching of an animal. Clinging to Henry, she pointed toward the sound. "What could that be?"

Grabbing a washing stick, Henry crept to the corner of the room and lifted a towel. A large, white chicken shot toward him, his two boney, wrinkled feet scrambled across the mess of socks and feathers, his beak ready to tear at Henry's slick hair.

"Run!"

Ruby turned to the doorway, but her feet slipped on the feathers strewn across the flooring. Henry threw her arm over his shoulder. They scrambled from the room like two soldiers fleeing the battlefield.

In the hallway they rammed Mrs. Worthington, who carried a box of thread. The thin lines of blue, green, and yellow threads unraveled as they shot through the air and rolled along the tiled hallway to the kitchen.

"Ahh!" Mrs. Worthington yelled as the angry chicken ran past, pecking at the wooden spools rolling from the scene.

The frantic flapping of the bird's wings left a trail of feathers to the dining room. Henry tugged off his slick socks and raced after the fowl, grasping for its neck and tipping the drink cart.

Henry knelt to the bird trapped in the corner of the room, trying to read its thoughts. Normally, he didn't consider the wayward thoughts of chickens, but desperation was the moment's emotion. The chicken's calm glare exposed his defiance. *It's angry at Billy for disturbing his breakfast.*

"If you let me," Henry said, "I will put you back outside, and you can be free."

Squatting low, he reached for the chicken who pecked at his hands and squawked its disapproval of the plan. Ruby jerked the delivery door open, and Henry tossed the bird to the yard. It dashed away, disappearing into the firebushes' orange blooms. Ruby closed the door and trudged to the table where Henry untied the knots of the laces.

"Can you believe the work the boys put into this one?" Ruby asked. "They certainly are good at what they do."

"It makes me want to be young again. To take life with a good bit of humor."

Mrs. Worthington stepped from the hallway, hands clasped at her waist and feathers stuck in her hair. "I'm sorry. I'll go find the boys."

ERNEST WOKE AND WIPED THE SWEAT DRIPPING FROM HIS hair. His eyes shot from the dresser to the window and back at his own hands. *I'm in my home on the estate*.

Dreams of his old apartment and its roach-infested walls haunted him as he adapted to his new tiny life. The dreams each night only made it harder for him to accept he might never return to normal—the normal before the potion turned him into a monster.

He slid from the flower-patterned blanket and toddled to the closet, yawning and stretching. The stitching and quality of the new suit still impressed and gave him a sense of pride in owning such luxury.

Stepping into the suit, he examined its fit in the sticker mirror on the wall. His image distorted along the pits and bumps of the shiny metal surface, but it didn't matter. He felt good from the inside out.

Ernest sauntered back to his bed and tucked the pillow under the covers. *If I'm to live here for much longer, I need to change some things to make it more comfortable.*

He leaned out the bedroom window and scowled at the lamp on George's desk. All night and all day, it shone on his bed like the sun on a hot summer day. This would be the first change.

The plastic ends of the bed frame screeched across the floor, creating a tight walkway between the tall dresser and the bed. Ernest moved the dresser into the closet where the snug fit allowed the doors to close.

After jogging down the stairwell decorated with striped wallpaper, he eyed the kitchen's appliances. The fridge and oven were made of balsa wood, and the doors didn't even open. *What good are these? I need real appliances, and that calls for electricity.*

Hanging his jacket over the kitchen chair, he rolled up his sleeves and marched out the back door. Strolling along the shelf stacked with boxes and glass containers, Ernest leaned backward and read the label of a smaller metal container. "Christmas."

Climbing up the decorative trim of the shelf, he jumped into the box of wires. Tangled and unlabeled, he spent most of the morning digging out the ones with tiny bulbs on the end, often used in the Christmas villages strung along mantles in well-to-do homes. Ernest rolled each one around his shoulder and secured them with a piece of tape.

Hiking across the shelf, he passed the last set of chemistry books and tossed the stringed lights to the front step of his home. He removed the tape from each cord and dragged them into the house one at a time.

By midafternoon, most rooms in the house had a light bulb, with the wires securely held behind the furniture using a stapler. Even by Ernest's standards, the bulbs were rather large, so he tucked them in the corner of each room, saving space. A single wire connected to the others stuck out the back window and dropped to the shelf.

Ernest lifted the plug and dragged it to the wall. Being mindful of the electricity pulsing through the line, he shoved it into the socket and glanced back at the home. Nothing happened.

Following the cord through the kitchen window, he found the gear switch near the middle of the wire. He stretched both arms inside and gripped the wheel, flicking on the lights. The whisper of an electrical charge hummed from the house.

Ernest admired his handiwork. Light poured from each window, creating a checkered pattern on the shelf. Walking into the kitchen, the single bulb in the room nearly blinded him, turning his vision to black, minus the shape of the bulb burned into his retina. A knock at the door had him feeling his way to the front entry, shuffling his feet as he went.

"Hello? Anyone home?"

Opening the door, the floral scent introduced Mrs. Worthington. "You have lights. How exciting."

"You'd think. I might have to take them out before I lose my vision."

Lowering her eyes to the curtainless windows, she peeked at his lighting setup. "Oh, no. All you need are lampshades.

I'll make some to fit over the bulbs. Something manly. No tassels or flowers."

"Could you?" Ernest walked from the doorway and leaned against a coffee mug holding pencils. "You know how to sew small clothes and make lampshades? It's just a hypothesis, but I suspect I might not be the only tiny person you've met."

"Don't be silly. I used to make all of Dink's doll items. That reminds me." Mrs. Worthington reached into her pocket. "I've brought you a gift. Just a little something I stitched up last night."

A short pile of seat cushions slipped from her fingers to the shelf. Ernest squeezed the soft pads covered in woolen fabric. A gold button in the center of each kept the stuffing from shifting. "These will fit my chairs perfectly."

"Oh, and this one."

"A mattress? I've been sleeping on wood all this time." Overwhelmed at her generosity, he pushed her hand away. "I couldn't."

"But you're the only person who could use them. I spent so much time making them especially for you."

"Well," he scratched his neck, "I wouldn't want you to have wasted your time. I'll take them. Thank you. Also, for the suit."

Mrs. Worthington grabbed a stool, folding her hands in her lap. "I see you wore it today, but perhaps you need work clothes. Something more flexible and breathable. I'm making some for George." Her eyes lit up. "Oh, I've got just the thing! The catalogue I order from has a new fabric with tiny fish. A very fun look for the summer."

"Why are you doing this for me?"

"It's my job. I'm the estate seamstress."

"Oh, I see," he looked away.

"And because you're my friend."

Ernest dangled his legs from the shelf. No one, not even his mother, had taken such an interest in his well-being. His younger years were spent questioning every good deed. No one acted out of pure kindness. Mrs. Worthington was different, and he wanted to repay her gentleness, but how?

"Say, do you need a tiny man in your workroom? I can fetch things dropped between cabinets and fit inside small spaces."

"As a matter of fact, I have a special machine for sewing coats. It has a thick needle. I haven't used it in years because of a tangled bobbin in the base. Maybe you could find the problem and get it working again?"

"It's worth a try. Do you have the manual?"

"Yes, I do. I'll make you lampshades and clothes if you fix my bobbin."

"Deal. I'll stop by later today and have a look at the machine."

"See you then." Mrs. Worthington swayed to the door and bent to Bruce the Loyal, whispering a kind word to him before climbing the stairs.

Ernest turned back to his house and scanned the light bursting from the windows. *Maybe I'll leave them off until after the shades are done. Now, on to indoor plumbing.*

DASHING ACROSS THE ICY FLOOR TO THE WARM BLANKETS OF her bed, Sophie Mae curled on the softness of the mattress. Outside her window, a cardinal bounced along the branches of the tree, chirping the day's chores or maybe the location of the full bird feeders in town.

A rhythmic tapping on the door signaled the start of her day. "Come in."

Dink bounced into the room and hopped to the bed, curling up next to Sophie Mae. "Mr. Kimall called. He's on his way. You better get dressed or no breakfast for you."

"Are the kids awake?"

"Yep, and you know James loves to eat."

Sophie Mae tossed off the blankets and hurried to the closet, pushing the hung clothes to the far left where she kept her Saturday choices. Made of heavy cotton and wool, they were durable enough for the Hooverville.

"Could you save me a muffin? I won't be long."

Dink saluted. "Yes, sir."

Alone in the enormous room, Sophie Mae changed into her work clothes and slid on her pair of work boots. They fit well. Her toes didn't ache from being squished, and the laces were so long, they wrapped around the top half of the boot twice.

A queasiness struck her gut as the floor of the bedroom transformed into coarse sand. The flapping of a yellow curtain hanging in a busted window told her she wasn't in the estate. Sitting on a wooden floor layered in dust, a thin, frayed shoestring wrapped her fingers. Her sore-covered hands reached for the bed, but a loud banging returned her to the cozy bedroom of the Gardenia Estate.

"Kimall's here, dumb girl." Billy's head rose along the crack of the ten-foot door. Tapping trailed along the wall as he moved down the hallway, floating to the stairs.

Sophie Mae tied the boot and raced to the door, looking back to the room. *That was like something out of the imagination room. How could that be? Maybe it was a memory from my past?*

Recoiling at the stairs' sticky handrail, she jogged into the kitchen following the scent of fresh bread. Dink sat on the counter, laughing and waving a muffin in the air. James whined and grabbed at the treat, begging for a bite. Dink looked to Sophie Mae and tossed her the muffin. "It's about time. This kid is relentless."

Sophie Mae stuck her thumbs into the bread and split it in half. She knelt to James. "I know it's hard to understand, but you don't need to horde food any longer. You don't need to beg."

"Yes, ma'am," he said, taking the food and running into Mr. Kimall at the delivery door. "Excuse me, sir."

"Whoa, little man! Where's the fire?" he chuckled, noticing the girls in the kitchen. "Y'all ready to go? I got the truck loaded."

Dink hopped from the counter and ran outside to the truck. Sliding to the middle of the truck's bench seat, she held her legs flat against the cushion, making room for the three-foot stick shift with the metal ball top.

Sophie Mae crawled into the passenger seat next to Dink, rolling the handle of the glass window. The truck roared to life. Mr. Kimall slammed on the gas, and they sped to the main street and out to the highway.

"No more gravel roads on the way to the village," Mr. Kimall yelled over the wind rushing into the cab. "I'll tell you what, this new work program from the government is great. The roads are smooth, and there's a new ball stadium downtown. Why, if I weren't an old man, I'd join those CCC boys."

"Those boys in the woods?" Dink asked.

"They ain't just in the woods. They're making trails and building bridges; but more importantly, they're saving the drought lands by irrigating and planting trees and brush."

There it was again. Sophie Mae cringed at the concerned

glance from Mr. Kimall. Whenever the topic of droughts and the dust bowl came up, people assumed Sophie Mae would have a brilliant tidbit to add. Though she'd witnessed the man-made disaster from the farm in Drycrop, the traveling box had stolen those memories, freeing her of the emotional distress.

The stretch of highway changed from farmlands to the shanty village of the Hooverville. Mr. Kimall parked the truck under the shade of a half-dead tree. Piling out of the cab, both girls picked up a wooden box full of fruits and vegetables.

Mr. Kimall adjusted his hat and overalls. "We'll start on the east side and work our way back to the truck. Stay together. I don't need to be on Catherine's bad side should something happen."

Sophie Mae's arms stretched under the crate's weight, and the wooden sides bumped against her legs. A group of kids playing jacks on an old wooden sign ran toward the thumping crate, taking fruit off the top. A young girl, small from years of malnourishment, waved. "Hi, Miss Sophie."

"Good morning, Josie. I have something special for you." Sophie Mae moved the oranges aside and grabbed the bag of strawberries. "Here you go."

Josie hugged Sophie Mae and ran back to the wooden sign, spreading the strawberries along the chipped paint logo. The kids feasted while waiting their turn at the game.

"You spoil her," Dink said. "If word gets around you have strawberries, there'll be a riot."

Mr. Kimall stepped to the first shack and tapped gently on the wall. Anything harder might have collapsed the entire building of weathered wood and sheets of used metal. The toothless grin of an older woman appeared from the curtained doorway.

"You're here. Come in. Come in." The woman laid a potholder made from reclaimed fabric into his crate. "I've made this for you."

"Thanks, but it's unnecessary. We bring food as a gift."

"It is most necessary for a trade, is it not?"

"I suppose you're right, and I do need one. I burnt the last one to ashes trying to cook a meatloaf."

Kimall tucked the gift into his pocket and handed the woman a few oranges and a pear. Smiling, she placed them into a hanging basket in the room's corner.

Sophie Mae tapped Mr. Kimall's shoulder. "Might I go next door and visit with Mrs. Baker? I promise to stay there until you arrive."

"Make sure you do, little miss. I know you're an adult now, but this place can be dangerous, and you know I promised Catherine I'd—"

"I know," Sophie Mae said. She patted Dink on the shoulder and slunk out of the shack.

Stepping lightly in the fresh mud, she thought about the plight of the villagers. Most were families displaced by economic hardship, like Mrs. Baker. The older woman lost her husband to the Great War and her home to the droughts. In the Hooverville, she found a new family connected by their shared struggles.

"Oh, child! Let me look at you." Mrs. Baker pored over every freckle on Sophie Mae's face, brushing her hair off her ear.

"How have you been?" Sophie Mae asked.

"Oh, you know how it goes, dear. Some days are better than others, like today. You've come and brought a blessing."

Sophie Mae reached into the crate for celery, tomatoes, and a handful of onions. Mrs. Baker's eyes grew at the bounty. "Yes, good. Save those sweet fruits for the young. Us old folks ain't got no need for them anymore."

A delicate bowl with gold accents dressed up an old barrel used as a table. Mrs. Baker gently placed the vegetables inside before sitting cross-legged on a handmade rug. "Tell me, how are Betsy and the kids doing?"

"She has gotten a job in the city at the general store. The days are long for her, but she seems happy. James is being taught to read at a local schoolteacher's home. Judy will join him next year when she turns four."

"And have there been any strange visitors? Anyone you don't trust?"

Sophie Mae worried at the woman's change in tone, strained and less jovial than usual. "Not that I've seen."

"Good, good. And how's that Billy? He'll make a fine man one day."

"Why do you ask about strangers?"

Mrs. Baker clasped her hands. "I don't like to think ill of people. We all have trials to overcome."

"And?"

"A man has been scouring the village. He peeks into our homes. We might not have doors with locks on them, but it don't make it proper." She brushed a fly resting on her forehead. "This man stopped me one day and asked if I knew his sister. I told him no. He showed me a picture from his wallet and can you believe it was Betsy? He was really irritated I didn't give him what he wanted."

"Did he say why he was looking for her?"

"Not a word, that's why I kept quiet. You never know these days."

"Knock, knock," Mr. Kimall said, standing at the door with Dink.

A broad smile covered Mrs. Baker as she greeted him with a hug. "My dear friend. Please come inside. Don't worry about the mud on your boots. There really ain't no way around it."

"I have a bag of oranges and pears for you."

"You can give those to Mrs. White," she balked, "but I'll have Lillian's bag of okra."

Dink passed the bag and Mrs. Baker pinched her cheek. "My, you have grown."

As Mr. Kimall and Dink moved on to the next house, Sophie Mae gave Mrs. Baker one last hug. "Please be careful."

"I'm always careful," Mrs. Baker said. "How do you think I got so old? Luck?" Her smile faded as she passed a gold ring to Sophie Mae. "Give this to Betsy. She wanted me to keep it, but I fear it's not safe with the man lurking about."

BRUNHOLD KNELT outside the Hooverville wall, watching Sophie Mae, the girl who asked too many questions about him. She hopped into the truck with the older man the locals called Kimall. While he applauded their desire to feed the hungry, they were a roadblock to him gaining the formula for his own people. The boisterous truck pulled from the shade to the main highway.

Brunhold hustled to his vehicle. Hurried and anxious, he forgot to shut the car door, which slammed into his shin. Jerking his leg inside the cab, he sped off the gravel parking lot and clutched the wheel, ready to chase the driver and find the house with the flowers sheltering Betsy.

The flood of adrenaline was wasted as Kimall drove slower than a line of tanks in a parade, hanging his arm out the window and waving to passing cars.

Following them through the town of Evenland, Brunhold got the long, scenic tour of the city. They passed the neglected school building, closed for lack of funding. Not much farther were two parallel shopping strips, divided by the roadway. A blue sign sat cheerfully on the right.

Welcome to Downtown Evenland
Enjoy Your Stay
Curfew 9:00 p.m.

Locals wandered the streets with bags and boxes, dodging the homeless lying on the street corners begging for work. Two left turns, and the truck throttled at the gate of a large estate. Sophie Mae sprang from the cab, tugging the gate outward. A stick dredged through the gravel making a line where the girls took a runner's stance.

"Ready, set, go!" Sophie Mae said as they dashed to the red brick home. Kimall drove slowly through the gate, leaving it open.

This must be the place. That boy at the Hooverville said Betsy lives here. I'm impressed. The fool did well for herself.

Pocketing his keys, he slunk out of the seat toward the

estate. A fountain bubbled in the distance, and he ran towards it, finding the three-tiered lawn ornament in front of an ivy-covered gate. The chatter of people had him peeking at the girls who carried on joyously as if the pain in the world didn't matter to them.

Kimall squinted at the gate where Brunhold hid. "I'll be right back, Dink. I hear something. Might be those raccoons Ms. Catherine keeps on about."

Brunhold crouched behind the wall of ivy as Kimall grumbled, moving closer to the gate. Looking upward through the leaves, Brunhold saw the man tip his hat and scratch his head. "I'm getting old, hearing things that ain't there."

"Mr. Kimall!" Sophie Mae shouted from under the arched driveway. "Come see the cake Mrs. Worthington made for the church. It's chocolate *and* strawberry."

Brunhold brushed the leaves from his suit and watched as Kimall rushed back to the house. The gate's rusty hinges squealed as Brunhold wrenched it open. He jogged through the gate and across the yard, leaning close to the brick, watchful for people or traps left by the magician.

Talking and laughter came from the back of the house. He peeked around the corner to the field, and his jaw dropped at the beauty of the estate. Flowering bushes and a hedge maze exposed the home's frivolous luxuries.

Hiding behind the multitude of bushes and trees, the buzzing of bees had him plucking a pear from the lowest branch. He bit into the tender skin. Its sweet juice rolled passed his chin and dripped to his gray vest. For a brief moment, he nearly lost himself in the estate's grandness.

Suddenly, the earth trembled. He dropped the fruit and

wiped his face with his sleeve as a giraffe's head bobbed over the bush. The large mammal strutted to the greater field, where an elephant spoke to it. His understanding of the animal's language sent him tumbling to the grass.

"You must throw the ball to me, not deliver it," the pachyderm said. "Perhaps we should take a break in the shade until George returns to entertain us."

George—that's the magician. I'm in the right place.

"You should ask him for a new potion so we may converse once again." The elephant looked to the sky. "Be cautious. Gus is approaching."

Brunhold fell back on his heels when Gus flew overhead, dropping bits of confetti. *A talking elephant and a flying bear. What form of black magic does he know? Betsy says it's science and chemistry, but those disciplines can't make an elephant talk.*

The bear circled over the estate prompting Brunhold to hide. He dashed to a water well a few feet away and lifted the wooden lid. Climbing inside, it relieved him to find a small ledge holding the water bucket. He kicked it into the deep hole and pulled the cover over his head, leaving a crack to keep his eyes on the magical bear.

"And this concludes our matinee," Gus said, hovering in the air with outstretched paws. "Please join us tonight for the Apple Throwing Contest and a special performance by the most talented Mary Louise."

"Thank you, Gus," the elephant said, "but I will not be performing this or any evening. I am retired."

Brunhold could take no more of the musty well and climbed out onto the soft grass. Returning the lid, he ran alongside the house, hiding behind a tree as Kimall's truck raced to the main gate. Jumping over the side fence, Brunhold started down the busy street, seeing his car in the distance.

Magic or science, it makes no difference. If this George can make animals talk and fly, he can surely make a growth potion for a few plants. When I return home with the formula, I'll be the savior of my people.

Billy had lived with Leggy, the invisible giraffe, for years and never once considered her thoughtful. Silly and quiet, yes, but never capable of thinking for herself. Maybe this was because she didn't voice her opinions as Mary Louise did.

Kicking the larger rocks from the garden path, he turned to James, who skipped next to him. "What made you wonder if Leggy had her own thoughts?"

James looked at Billy. "Mary Louise always tells us what Leggy wants, like Mom does to me. She tells me I love baths, but I don't. What if Leggy doesn't want to take a bath, and Mary Louise says she does?"

Scratching his chin, Billy nodded. "You might be on to something, little man."

"So…so, we take Leggy to the imagination room and tell her to think of whatever she wants."

Billy strode in thoughtful silence while James glanced at him every other step. It bothered him he hadn't thought of the scheme first. *Am I slacking as the troublemaker of the house?*

"We have to do this, James. It should've been done long ago."

"Leggy will be so happy," James said. "Can we tell her now?"

"Sure. I'll give you a monkey ride."

James wasted no time jumping to the boy's leg and to his shoulders. His small, muddy feet wrapped around Billy's back and kicked him in the side. "Giddy-go!"

Billy proudly galloped across the field, dodging trees and small critters digging for grubs. He stopped at the clearing and gazed at Mary Louise and Leggy, whose eyes glossed over watching the pink-tipped grass sway in the wind.

"Look how sad they are," Billy said. "Leggy needs to go to the imagination room before she dies of boredom."

James agreed, nodding faster than a kid on a sugar rush. Scrambling from Billy's shoulders, he dropped to the field and raced toward the lounging animals. He slipped on the dewy grass and landed next to Mary Louise, who picked the sticky weeds from his feet with her trunk. "Good afternoon, James."

"Good afternoon, Mary Louise," he copied.

"What are you and young Billy doing today?"

Billy huffed. "Why do you always ask him about my

plans? I can talk for myself. You can't put words into my mouth like you do with everyone."

"I can see that."

James jumped to his feet. "And you can't tell Leggy what to do, either." Hugging Mary Louise's trunk, he fell to the mountain of her torso.

"I wonder if I have this correct?" Mary Louise asked. "You believe I tell others what they want and how to live. Is that close?"

Billy reached out his hand for James. "Come on. Let's go to the barn and jump from the hayloft."

James crawled from Mary Louise and kissed her trunk. "Bye-bye. I'll be back after, and you can tell me a story about tigers."

"Goodbye, James," Mary Louise said. "What a fine young man."

Billy and James ran to the barn, kicking up dirt along the path. Their palms slapped the rungs of the ladder leading to the loft where they dived into the haystack. "We need a plan," Billy said. "With Mary Louise around, we'll never get Leggy to the room."

The first hurdle would be separating the two animals. Billy knew they spent the mornings together. Mary Louise chased the wild bunnies while Leggy ate most everything she could find. In the afternoon, they slept under the shade of a tree.

Nightfall proved their only chance.

"They sleep on opposite sides of the barn because Leggy snores," Billy thought out loud. "We could take her through the back door of the barn after Mary Louise falls asleep."

James squinted his eyes like Billy. "And she's invisible, so it'll be easy to herd her up the stairs."

"She's not invisible to the others in the house."

"But sometimes she hides in the trees, and I can't see her."

Billy rolled his eyes. James's pranking had improved, but sometimes the limits of his age got in the way. No one told the young boy of the potion, claiming he was too young to understand. Billy continued with his idea. "Tonight when the sun sets, we'll take Leggy from the barn and bring her to the imagination room. Right now, we gather supplies."

A LARGE DOGWOOD TREE, nearly white from shedding its bark, grew behind the barn. Its hefty branches were perfect for hiding. Billy and James scooted up the trunk, legs dangling as the pink sky faded into deep black.

Digging through the bag on his shoulder, Billy listed the supplies for the third time since they scaled the tree. "Rope for her neck, peanut butter, the sheet from my bed, and two pairs of slippers, one from Langston's room and the other from George's."

"And I got chewing gum," James cheered, pulling the warm and squishy treat from his pocket.

"What's the gum for?"

"In case she cries from missing Mary Louise."

"Good thinking."

Billy lowered his eyes as George approached carrying a large basket of fruit. Ambushed by Gus Grizzly, the bear stole a treat and flew into the barn. Minutes later, George paraded from the barn with the empty basket, waving his free hand as if he were conducting an orchestra playing in his mind.

"That's our cue," Billy said.

Finding their footing among smaller branches, the boys dropped to the tall grass. Billy led the younger James to the barn, then pressed his ear to the wood. The heavy breathing of a drowsy Mary Louise vibrated the door. When the slight whistling of her trunk started, Billy nodded to James.

The wood plank barring the back exit of the barn lifted quickly. Billy swung the wide door open a few inches, and the jagged bottom scraped the dirt and rocks.

"Careful," James squeaked.

Billy held a finger to his lips, shushing him. A small lantern hung from a hook and lit the first level of the barn. Mary Louise was curled in her usual spot next to Gus, but Leggy was missing.

A burst of soggy air blanketed Billy's shoulder. He toppled to the swaying grass while James hugged the giraffe's long neck.

"How'd you do that?" Billy whispered to Leggy, who chuckled.

James laughed. "She can't talk, silly."

"Right. Let's go."

The route to the house proved more exciting, cloaked in the darkness of night. Leggy zigzagged through the garden as the boys bounced along her back, struggling to hold on. Though Billy loved adventure, he preferred knowing the obstacles in his path.

Leggy padded to the doors of the dining room, and the first problem revealed itself as she ducked her head to sniff the door handle.

"She's so tall," James pointed out. "She won't fit through."

Billy scratched his ear, not sure what to do. He paced the brick-laid patio. *How do you get a giraffe into a house? It sounds like a riddle.*

James tugged at Billy's shirt as Leggy pressed her long snout against the brick, passing through as if the structure was built of smoke. The length of her neck disappeared into the wall, followed by her torso. Her fluffy tail flipped outside the bricks for a few seconds before it too disappeared. *She can pass through walls?*

Pushing the glass door open, James ran inside the foyer of the home. Billy scrambled behind him, not prepared for the giraffe standing tall enough to sniff the chandelier hanging above the stairs.

Clamoring to her back, James kicked Leggy in the side. "Up and at 'em!"

CLOP-CLOP-CLOP

As Leggy tromped to the stairs, her hooves hit the floor and echoed through the giant room. Billy held her neck, stopping her from waking the entire house. The two sets of slippers from his bag had to be wrestled away from Leggy, who grabbed them with her teeth.

"No," Billy said, marching around the animal and sliding the slippers to her hooves. "Now, up you go."

The first step on the stairs creaked under her weight. They froze and waited for the adults to come yelling from their rooms.

Silence.

James held tight to Leggy's neck as Billy marched in front, leading them with the rope to the third floor's landing. Billy leaned over the railing, scanning for his mother while concocting a fib to cover their plan, if needed. With the coast clear, he turned to Leggy, who licked the dead flies from the wall sconces. "All you got to do is open the door. The room will find your most favorite memory."

Leggy tapped her slipper-covered foot on the floor and clutched the door handle with her teeth. The tall paneled door creaked open, and the kids peeked inside. Billy frowned at the scene developing in the imagination room. Banners for sideshows and rides appeared along the main path. "The circus. Oh, man! Why is it always the circus?"

The farther Leggy strolled along the wood deck, the more being there felt wrong. James slid off her back and grabbed Billy's hand. "I'll keep you safe from the clowns."

As the circus lights sprang to life and food carts churned out sweet aromas, the crowd appeared. The first giraffe wore a green hat and Mary Jane shoes large enough to fit over her hooves. Her husband, or so Billy thought, appeared wearing a bow tie at the top of the neck, just under his chin. Wide, wing-tipped shoes matched the style.

James laughed and skipped with excitement as giraffes of all sizes populated the walkways of the circus. Billy was confused. *Giraffe people? Is this really what Leggy thinks about? A world filled with other giraffes?*

Rubbing snouts with passing giraffes, Leggy appeared to be at home. She sniffed a poster tacked to a wooden fence. It read 'The Amazing Eric' and had a sketch of a giraffe in a top hat and cape. The one nailed next to it showed a human jumping through a ring of fire, complete with a tie and briefcase.

"This place is great!" James said. "Giraffes everywhere."

Surrounded by giraffe families and rebellious-looking

teenage calves, Billy trod lightly, hoping they didn't notice he and James were human.

Screams shot from behind Billy as dozens of giraffes whizzed by on the wooden roller coaster, their necks in tall, supportive restraints. A brightly colored booth sold light-up toys and gadgets. A young calf examined a pair of purple blinking earrings dangling to her shoulders.

Leggy took a few steps and stopped at the Buttery Corn stand, where an overflowing bucket of popcorn sat on the counter. Sliding a ticket to the old giraffe working inside, Leggy ducked her head under the handle. It rested between her ears and short horns, allowing her to walk and eat her snack.

Billy moved along with the crowd feeling something wasn't quite right. He wiped his eyes. All the food carts served popcorn, though each had a unique name. A giraffe could have a necklace of stringed popcorn from Ring-o-Snack or a crazy popcorn hat molded like a human from the Corny Adventures cart for a single ticket. James took a stringed popcorn necklace from the hook and lobbed it over his head. He pointed in the distance. "Leggy's running away!"

The sea of spots and necks made finding her difficult. Billy squinted as he searched the crowd. "Which way did she go?"

"This way." James ran along the wood boardwalk. Billy followed. Giraffes snapping photos along the bridge and those using the stationary binoculars shook their hooves at the boys darting and dodging their way to the other side.

"A human broke out of his cage!" one yelled, pointing his hoof at them. Giraffe mothers clutched their calves and worried as Billy and James scampered past.

"There!" Billy said, clearing the mass of giraffes. Leggy stood at the end of the boardwalk and stared at an older giraffe alone in a grassy field. "Do you think they know each other?"

James shrugged as he munched on his necklace.

Stepping lightly through the grass, Leggy spoke. "Bisa? Mother, is that you?"

Billy covered his mouth at Leggy's deep voice, his gut churning. *She can speak. I hope she doesn't remember all the times I harassed her.*

"Delu? My precious Delu? This can't be real." The mother ran to Leggy and licked the red patches of hair on her head.

"Delu!" James said. "That's Leggy's real name!"

Banners and yellow lanterns hanging from hooks faded as the boardwalk changed from wooden deck to the hay-covered floor of an animal cage. The lively circus spectacular turned into a dark and lonely night in the middle of nowhere.

Billy held James's hand as they approached the cage reeking of animal dung. The closer they stepped, the more James gripped. Kneeling next to him, Billy placed his hand on his shoulder. "I don't know what's going to happen. It might be scary. We can turn back."

"We need to stay so we can help Leggy," James said.

A young calf cuddled in the hay by her mother. Billy could tell it was Leggy by her eyelashes. Bisa cleaned Leggy's fur with her long tongue. Despite their lack of water and food, they sat in peace.

"Come find me when you're older, my dear Delu," Bisa said.

At once, Billy felt nauseous as an animal trainer stepped through Billy's body, as if he were nothing but a mist. James tugged Billy's hand and examined his face. "Billy?"

He forced a courageous smile.

Unlocking the cage, the trainer climbed inside and marched to the small giraffe family huddled in the corner. He took a rope from his belt and threw it around Leggy's neck. "I can't believe they're selling off this one. Training the creatures young works out best for everyone." Outside the cage, Leggy fought against him. "I don't make the rules. Time to go."

Bisa stepped to the bars of the cage and sniffed her calf's scent. Leggy moaned and hummed as they dragged her to a waiting farm truck. Three large men shoved her inside and locked the trailer door. Two bangs on the rear panel and billows of smoke hid their escape.

Being in the imagination room, Leggy reappeared in her normal form next to Billy, who reached to comfort her. James moved faster and hugged Leggy's neck.

The room changed for the third time, and they found themselves in the field of the Gardenia Estate. The time of day had shifted, and the sun in the bright sky nearly blinded them. Leggy lifted James by his collar to her back, and the three of them headed to the familiar barn.

Mary Louise charged from the red doors as Leggy approached. It confused Billy. *If her mother is in the circus, why does she want to see Mary Louise?*

"How did the potion go, Delu? Are you feeling any pain?" Mary Louise asked.

"I feel normal, but I understand the human's noises. Why does the man call me Leggy?"

"Most likely due to your long legs."

"If he deems the name suitable, I suppose I'll keep it. It's less of a reminder of my mother."

"As you wish," Mary Louise said. "Would you care to join me for lunch in the orchard?"

Billy watched as the two old friends meandered to the peach trees, both fresh from taking the potion. Leggy took a sniff of the ripe fruit and bit into the skin, swallowing hard. A humming and growling came from her throat as she attempted to comment on the sweetness of the fruit.

Mary Louise dropped the fruit from her trunk and ran to her friend's side. "Leggy. What is happening?"

Trying hard to speak, the growling continued. Her hoof beat the ground as she grew impatient.

"Oh, dear, this cannot be good." Mary Louise panicked and let out a loud trumpet toward the Gardenia House.

A much younger George raced for the animals. With a spring in his step, he still wore the same old magician clothes.

"What's the matter?" George the Great asked. "Leggy doesn't look good."

"It is the potion. It has cursed her."

George looked around the ground and found the half-eaten peach. "Is this hers?"

"This is no time to criticize her food choices," Mary Louise balked. "You must help."

George moved to Leggy and laid his head to her chest, counting the beats of her heart, which had normalized. The giraffe licked his hair as she always had, as if she'd forgotten her brief ability to speak

"Delu?" Mary Louise asked. "Leggy? Do you understand me?"

Leggy nodded, rolling her tongue from her mouth.

"She's still invisible," George said, twirling his mustache. "And she looks fine."

"Leggy cannot speak. Make her talk again."

"I'm afraid I can't, at least not at the moment," George said. "Eating has stripped her ability to communicate with us. I'll need time to study the side effects of the potion. For now, she's not showing any signs of distress."

"Leggy, can you hear me?" Mary Louise called.

The giraffe hummed low.

Billy turned to James. "So, that's why she can't talk like Mary Louise."

"Oh, I knew that already," James said.

"How?"

"Mary Louise told me under the story tree."

"Oh."

Leggy cleared her mind, and the imagination room returned to its normal state. She walked for the door, seeming to understand how the room worked.

"That was strange," Billy said walking to the hallway. "We best get her back to the barn before anyone notices."

"Yesterday I went with Betsy and the kids to the park," Dink said. "You'll never guess who I saw."

"Who?" Sophie Mae asked.

"Aren't you gonna guess? Even once?"

"Did you see…Billy?"

"Ugh! No. I saw Thomas, the boy who works at the hardware store."

"Thomas? Which one is he again?"

Sophie Mae grinned at Dink's pouty face as they walked along Main Street to Ronald's Bits and Bobs, the local fabric store. Sent by Mrs. Worthington, the girls were on a mission to find a single button to match the few remaining on James's coat.

As they passed Evenland Hardware, Dink stopped and pressed her head to the glass. "He's got to be at work today."

Sophie Mae giggled at Dink and continued along the sidewalk, stepping from the curb. The clicking of a woman's heels in the alleyway drew her attention. The woman's long, brown hair bounced as she hurried toward a dark figure standing by the fence in the back. Sophie Mae thought the woman might be Betsy, though she hoped to be wrong. She dashed to the brick building and peered around the corner, squinting for a better look at the couple in the alley.

Rays of sun scattered through the branches of a tree, illuminating the woman who now dabbed tears from her eyes. It was definitely Betsy. Her presence wasn't unusual as she worked in the general store a few doors down, but being in the alleyway was a different story. *What is she doing meeting someone in the alley? Could it be the man from the camp Mrs. Baker warned me about?*

Sophie Mae couldn't travel the narrow passage without being spotted. Instead, she craned her ear and closed her eyes to eavesdrop on their conversation. Her arm scratched along the rough brick as Dink popped up behind her. "What'cha doing?"

"Look in the alley."

"For what, exactly?" Dink asked.

Sophie Mae scanned the now empty alleyway. *Maybe they moved behind the building.*

Dink leaned against the building and wrangled her wayward hair. "I'd love to look at Thomas, but he wasn't in the store. That boy will never notice me."

"Maybe because you're invisible?" Sophie Mae smirked.

"You're so funny. I've made myself visible to him many times like I do when we go to the Hooverville. You know, we used to be classmates, but he doesn't recognize me at all."

Sophie Mae tugged Dink by the arm. "Come on. We've got a mission from the mother ship. Make yourself visible so I don't look like I'm talking to myself."

"Making you look odd is the best part of coming into town."

With Dink now visible, the girls entered the fabric store, and the owner hurried to them, dropping his gold-chained glasses to his chest. "Good afternoon. I'm Ronald. How might I be of service?"

Sophie Mae reached into her pocket and produced the worn black button. "I need one of these to match, please."

"Most certainly."

As the owner searched the rack of buttons, Sophie Mae and Dink admired a thimble decorated with roses and hearts, a collector piece for the community's older women.

"What do you know about Betsy?" Sophie Mae asked casually.

"Probably less than you. You knew her before I did."

"Right, but maybe your mother has said something in passing?"

Dink topped each of her fingers with the display thimbles and clanked them together. "She is 30 years old…"

"Yes."

"She has two kids…"

"James and Judy."

"Her husband left her stranded in the station because he's a bum and a good for nothing…"

"Your mom didn't say that, did she?" Sophie Mae wrinkled her nose.

"No, Ms. Ruby did during a fitting for a new apron. Now that I think about it, she also said Betsy was the daughter of a botanist, whatever that means. He lives in one of those asylums for people who hear voices."

"What about a brother or something?"

"Nope. At the park, Betsy told me she was an only child. She had two kids, so they'd always have each other and never be alone."

Ronald sang as he squeezed through the aisle to Sophie Mae. "Here you are, my dear. A perfect match, minus the scrapes and chips."

"Can you put it on my tab—Catherine Gardenia, please?"

"Most certainly. Ms. Gardenia has been a godsend to the town. Please give her my regards."

"Thank you, sir." Sophie Mae opened the door and Dink passed through first.

Walking toward the estate, the green-and-yellow awnings of the hardware store sheltered them from the migrating birds resting on the branches of a nearby tree. Dink stopped and took a last peek inside the store for Thomas. She turned from the window. "He's not there, but guess who is?"

"Dink..."

"All right. It's Betsy."

"In the hardware store?"

"No, in the ice cream parlor," Dink said sarcastically.

Sophie Mae shot to the window and saw Betsy in the cleaning section, scanning the liquid soaps. From around the aisle came the tall man from the alleyway. He stopped to examine the shelf behind Betsy. A white note passed from his hand to hers. The man strode to the shop's exit, leaving Betsy with tears in the quiet corner of the store. Tipping his hat to the cashier at the counter, he exited the doorway and made a sharp right past the shopping strip.

Sophie Mae tugged Dink behind a large mailbox.

"What's going on with you?" Dink asked. "You're so jumpy today."

"Come on," Sophie Mae said. "We have to follow him."

"I can go ahead of you, so we don't lose him," Dink said. "I'll put up my invisibility. He'll never know I'm there."

Dink weaved past the slower walkers and mothers with baby buggies, finally reaching a crowd hypnotized by the whooshing of traffic on the busy street. Sneaking behind the man, she flashed a thumbs up.

Sophie Mae sped toward Dink, halting when the man turned directly to Dink. *Her invisibility is up. How does he see her?*

Lost in the moment's confusion, Sophie Mae stumbled in front of two boys racing on their bicycles. The taller of the boys swerved from a small, leashed dog and hit her with his handlebars. Strangers helped Sophie Mae to her feet, and she ran for Dink, who stood frozen as the man spoke to her then hurried across the road.

Sophie Mae held her by the shoulders. "Are you okay?"

"He saw me."

"What happened?"

"He told me he knows about the magic, and I should be more careful."

A knot swelled in Sophie Mae's gut. *He knows about Mr. George and the others. Betsy gave us away?*

TUGGING AT HER EAR, BETSY IGNORED THE GUILT OF ONCE again leaving the kids in the care of Ms. Ruby. The woman was more than capable, but a child needs their mother. She quickened her pace along the pebble drive, focusing on her mission.

For two years, the estate had offered her relief from the worst of the depression. Sophie Mae saved them from poverty, transporting them to a dream world where food and drink no longer mattered, and animals held conversations about the weather. Though she'd never imagined such a place existed, it was a perfect landing for her and her kids.

Betsy darted across the busy street as if she were heading to work at the local general store. Bending to tie her shoe, she scanned the street for prying eyes, finding none. She hustled to the corner and glanced at the phone booth. Already occupied, she leaned against a brick wall to wait.

The small slip of paper she'd gotten from Brunhold lingered in her pocket, shredding her hope for a normal life. There was no need for her to read it for the hundredth time. She'd memorized its threat.

Get the chemist to make the potion
and I'll forget the kids exist.

"Oh, no." A woman stepped from the booth, tugging at her green skirt stuck in the hinges of the door.

"Allow me," Betsy said. Gently closing the door halfway, she teased the fabric from the hinge. The small dab of grease disappeared in the folds of the skirt.

"Thank you."

"Anytime," Betsy said, entering the booth, carefully shutting the door. She dropped a nickel from her pocket into the slot, and it clanked against the pile of coins collected in the money box.

One ring, then two.

Betsy tapped the handset. "Pick-up."

Three rings, then four.

"Hello?" a rough voice shouted through the line.

"Mother. It's me, Betsy."

"Betsy Ann? Is that you?"

"Yes, Mother. I'm calling to tell you I'm alright."

"You should be, living in that grand house. Are my grandkids hurt? Is that why you called?"

"No." Betsy covered the mouthpiece as she sighed. "I wanted to hear your voice."

"Then maybe you should come to visit. This telephone contraption distorts your words. How's that husband of yours? Has he found a job yet?"

"I haven't seen him in years, Mom," she lied. "I don't think I ever will."

"I suppose it's for the best. He was a bad seed. Always bothering your father about his work and how it could feed the world. And don't think I forgot his family lineage. Having a German in the family was embarrassing. The neighbors still ask about Brunhold."

"The Great War was twenty years ago, and it's time to move on. The German leadership was defeated morally and monetarily, what harm could they pose?"

"Mark my words, Betsy Ann, we've not seen the last of those warmongers."

"I have to go, Mom. Tell Dad I love him."

"I won't see him for two months. The clinic is too far away for me to travel alone. Even if I could, it wouldn't make a bit of difference. He can't remember what day it is, much less who you are. Why don't you do us both a favor and stay out of trouble?"

Betsy hung up the phone. Her temples pounded. Dropping her head to the receiver, she startled as a man in a business suit banged on the phone booth. Betsy gathered her bag and exited. "Apologies."

She entered the memorial park and claimed a bench with a

gold plate on the back, dedicating the seat to a local war hero. She took no notice of his name as tears fell. A handkerchief hid half her face and a bit of her shame from the public. *Why does Dad have to be sick? I need him so much right now.*

She traded the silk fabric for her father's Bible and rubbed a fallen tear from the cover. Not a religious family, her dad considered the book a great place to hide his life's work. 'People avoid the thing like the plague,' he used to say.

Holding the book loosely, a natural part revealed itself near the back where a folded map lay tucked inside. Betsy opened the delicate paper and searched for her next destination. She'd spent the last year searching rivers and parks for the elusive argan seeds her dad spoke of for the formula. Rundleville, the closest location, was a four-hour bus trip from Evenland and would be her real job for the day.

JUST A DROP or two of rain hit the bus's window as it drove along the two-lane highway. Betsy ran her fingers over the cold glass, following the water's descent to the window's rubber seal as it rolled down the slick glass, disappearing until it was forgotten.

Her dad, a brilliant botanist in his youth, understood the secret to food security was in the growing. The faster you grew food, the more you'd have. But like the drop of rain, his own mind dissipated and disappeared.

A road sign appeared in the distance.

Rundleville
5 miles

For the first time since her morning coffee, Betsy grinned. The bus slowed and the metal racks near the ceiling pinged as riders gathered their belongings. A sweeping left into the bus station tossed the early standers onto the laps of others.

The passengers filed out of the noisy metal beast to the concrete, where an awning shielded them from the misting rain. Betsy lurked behind the small ticket building for a little privacy and huddled inside a doorway. A closer inspection of the map convinced her to find a ride.

As people congregated around the benches and payphones, she spotted a lone man shoving a large suitcase into the trunk of a Chevrolet sedan. He dropped into the driver's seat, flinching as Betsy tapped on the window.

"Excuse me, sir," Betsy said. "Might I have a lift? I need to get to Goose Creek. It's not far from here."

"Sure thing, young lady. I'm passing right by the place. Hop inside."

Betsy opened the passenger door to a stack of books on the floorboard, hardbound with shimmering page edges. She hesitated to sit in the seat.

"I'm an encyclopedia salesman. Knowledge is power." He smiled confidently. "Just put your feet on top of them. Those are returned books. Exactly twenty-two pages are missing from each. What good is an encyclopedia that skips the market crash of 1929?"

With the windows rolled down, the automobile slunk from the parking lot. Betsy watched the bus disappear in the rearview mirror as they cruised along the road.

The wind rushed into the car, making small talk impossible, which suited Betsy. Majestic trees bordered the paved lanes, their crisp scent like that of the Gardenia House. *I hope the kids are doing okay. It's just as well Ms. Ruby is taking care of them. I won't be around much longer.*

Gravel wedged between the tread of the tires as they veered to the side of the highway. "Goose Creek," the man said with a smile.

"Thank you." Betsy opened the car door, got out, and waved at the man continuing on his way.

A thick tree line hid the forest's actual size, which only reached a few hundred yards deep to her destination, a pond. Betsy stepped into the trees. The soft dirt, concealed by leaves and fallen branches, threatened to swallow the heels of her shoes.

Spider webs and the rustle of woodland creatures told her to retreat, but she pressed onward. Emerging from the forest, she removed her shoes and plodded close to the bank of the pond. Mud squished into her stockings and between her toes.

Argania Spinosa grows in dry land. Why would dad think it's here?

Trusting the map, she searched for the shrubby tree. Hours passed. Nothing. Kicking the trunk of a sapling, she dropped to her knees and covered her face. *It has to be here, but I'm running out of time. I can't be late to the estate again. They'll ask questions.*

Defeated, she ventured back through the forest for the road. The return journey to the bus station was twenty minutes by car, and the highway hadn't a single vehicle for her to catch a ride. Wobbling along the loose gravel, she noticed a small tree with fruits. She yanked one from the branch and sniffed the skin. *Argan seeds! Now to get back to the house.*

MARY LOUISE DROPPED the handle of the large red wagon, and James and Judy clamored up the wooden sides, peeking over the rim. Sponges, brushes, and combs lay scattered along the bottom. James reached for the long handle of a push broom, lifting his torso over the side and losing his balance.

Billy raced to help the boy upright. "Don't let the size trick you," he said, twirling a used human toothbrush in his fingers. "The real fun comes with this. Wait until you see the disgusting things stuck between an elephant's toes."

Having spent a lifetime around young children in the circus, Mary Louise read the disappointment in James's eyes. She reached for the broom with her trunk and handed it to him. "Choose whichever you prefer. If you must use the long brush, hold it right here to balance out the weight."

James swung and dropped the broom over and over again as he wielded it like a sword. His weak arms gave no control over its motion. Billy threw a large stick at James's feet and challenged him to a duel with a large stick of his own. James tossed the broom, choosing to wield the stick sword. The battering of the duel drew in most of the residents, most of whom cheered for James.

Mary Louise's ears flapped at a slight yell from the red wagon. She tapped Sophie Mae on the shoulder. "I believe Judy needs assistance."

Grabbing Dink, they raced to Judy, who'd fallen headfirst into the cart. Judy's feet kicked, leaving little room for Sophie Mae to duck past and lift her to standing. Dusting the dirt from the child's nose, she asked, "What are you looking for?"

"I don't know," Judy shrugged. "Is there a pretty one?"

Dink lifted the pink sponge donated by Ms. Catherine. "What about this one? It makes Mary Louise smell like flowers."

"I want it. I want it!"

Shiny bubbles drifted along the breeze toward Judy, who jumped and clapped at them. Leggy trekked from the main house with a second wagon carrying a barrel of warm, sudsy water, the temperature set to Mary Louise's liking.

The liquid sloshed back and forth in the container as it parked next to the wagon with the cleaning supplies. George lifted the rope off Leggy's back and splashed his hand in the water, drenching her tail. She raced to the wagon and grabbed a tube of toothpaste with her teeth.

Mary Louise, usually a creature of quiet introspection, loved the chaos building around her. "Thank you all for coming out today to help George with my monthly bath."

"Enough talking," Billy said, thrusting the toothbrush into the sudsy barrel.

"It's bath time for you!" James threw his hands to his hips in a motherly fashion.

Mary Louise frowned and plopped to her hind legs. "If I must. Make sure you scrub behind my ears."

Judy climbed to Mary Louise's leg, then her head where she washed the bristly hairs forever stuck upwards. James flicked a towel, brushing the dust from her legs as a stream of sudsy water flowed from the deep wrinkles in her skin to the grass.

"Not so hard, Billy. Are you mining for gold?" Mary Louise asked. "Careful, Judy. We cannot pin my tail back in place like a party game donkey."

Leggy bellowed, shaking the toothpaste clutched in her teeth.

"Right," Billy said. "It's high time you cleaned those choppers."

Billy loaded the boar-hair toothbrush and held back Mary Louise's lips, shoving it to her teeth. Squirming and groaning, she tilted her head against the boy's powerful arm. Having her teeth brushed was the worst part of bath time.

George opened and closed a tiny pair of scissors as he approached Mary Louise. "Just a trim?" He clutched the end of her snout and drew out the long hairs around her nostrils into a ponytail. "Are you growing a mustache? Do you like mine that much?"

"Do as you must," Mary Louise said, with a fake scowl. Her heart lightened at the family who hustled to care for her needs. *Life has never been so good. I am surrounded by loved ones of all sizes.*

BARAGH!

Mary Louise flew to her hind legs at the sting of cold water on her back. Billy and James ran for the barn, laughing and howling. Mary Louise marched to the water trough swimming with beetles and grass, and filled her trunk.

Billy stopped at the slurping sound. "Uh-oh!"

The boys' quick footwork was no match for Mary Louise's strength and accuracy. Planting her feet, water blasted from her snout and across the field, leaving Billy and James dripping wet. Judy ran to her brother and scrubbed his arm with a dry cloth. "You're taking a bath outside!"

George climbed to Mary Louise and patted her back. "Attack, Captain Super Soaker!"

Mary Louise refilled her trunk and padded around the

barn to the faint giggle of girls hunkered down behind the red tractor. Dink, frightened by Mary Louise's expression, rushed behind Sophie Mae. Judy cowered behind both of them. Six pairs of nervous eyes begged Mary Louise to reconsider.

"Wait!" Sophie Mae yelled, but it was too late. A stream of mucus-mixed water bombarded the two older girls while Judy ran for the tree line, slightly wet.

"Yee-haw!" George said, swirling his hand like a cowboy with a trick rope.

Mary Louise jogged after Judy, and the quick pace of the chase left her out of breath. Everything stopped when the child clung to her mother's leg.

"What's going on?" Betsy asked. "I heard screaming."

"Everything is fine. Just having a little fun." George slid from Mary Louise's back, stumbling as Betsy pulled him toward the trees.

Mary Louise watched with concern as Betsy muttered to George and pointed to the chaos happening on the field, apparently unaware elephants had fantastic hearing.

"What are you doing, George? Did you make progress on the potion?"

"Not yet, but I can feel it's getting close."

She straightened the collar of his shirt. "This work is important to me. If I were as smart and clever as you, I'd do it myself."

"I'm glad you're not…because I enjoy helping you."

Betsy moved closer to George. "To the lab, then?"

"Of course." George marched across the field. "Everyone, I'm calling it a day. James and Judy, you need a bath before dinner."

Groans of displeasure at being dismissed didn't help their cause. George strutted away and didn't even say goodnight.

Mary Louise's trunk dropped. She turned her attention to Betsy. The wet sock party crasher stepped along the grass, picking up sponges and dropping them into the bucket as she moved closer to Mary Louise. "I can't believe I missed the fun," Betsy said with a fake frown. "It's too bad I have to work."

"Perhaps we should schedule a time for you to join us. I am certain James and Judy would enjoy having you here."

"You're such a distraction," she said. "George wastes his time washing an elephant that will only re-dust herself, and now you want me to sit idle? I'm afraid I haven't the time. Why, work was so busy, I skipped lunch."

Mary Louise grinned. "There is food in nearly every tree. Might I suggest the peaches? They are ripe enough to be sweet and still crunchy."

"I think I will." Betsy reached for the highest peach in the tree. "Could you help me out, Mary Louise?"

Walking to the tree, Mary Louise noticed the lower hanging peaches were easily within Betsy's grasp. *She tempts me with fruit? Perhaps she desires to fade my potion.*

"This one?" Mary Louise asked, pointing her snout. She plucked the peach with the two finger-like ends of her trunk, lowering it to Betsy. "I am certain you will love it."

"Would you like to share?"

"No, thank you."

"George tells you food fades the potion because he doesn't want to share with you. He lies to protect the food for us humans."

"George does not lie."

"Believe what you will. I only wanted to warn you of his true intentions." Betsy bit hard into the peach and wiped the juice from her chin, dropping the wasted fruit.

As Betsy strutted to the house, Mary Louise squinted. Her lie about George was the final bit of information she needed. *We cannot trust Betsy. Her games will not bode well for the children.*

BILLY FLOATED TO THE STAIRCASE'S RAILING AND LOOMED over the foyer like a bald eagle guarding its dominion. Brandishing an imaginary sword, he coasted along the rail, jumping and twisting in the air. Landing on the first floor, he tugged his cap from his back pocket and crammed it on his head.

Racing outside the house through the wide doors of the dining room, Billy thought about his big plans for the day, the first of which was picking up his honorary little brother. Watching James grow up from being a young kid gave him great pride. He wanted to be the one to teach him everything a boy needed to know, but there didn't seem to be enough time in the day with fishing, trap setting, and swimming.

Billy ran along the pebbled pathway, kicking the rocks with his worn shoes. The cottage was over the hill, so he slowed to straighten the collar of his shirt and pat his hair down the middle of his head. He knocked on the front door and threw on a cheesy smile.

Betsy opened the door, hugging him tight as if the floor was dissipating. "I'm glad to see you. James is running around the house, playing pretend chicken. Please say you've come to take him?"

"I have, ma'am."

"Great," she said, nearly falling as James sprinted past her out the door.

Billy turned to chase the boy when Betsy grabbed his arm. "You'll take care of him, right? He's my only boy."

"Yes, ma'am. I'll treat him like a kid brother."

Billy ran after James, but the kid was faster and vanished in the tall weeds. Parting the grass with his hands, Billy searched for the trail of trampled foliage. Nothing. A screeching came from the left, and James soared into the air. *Can he float, too?*

Running toward the laughter, Billy frowned as Mary Louise tossed the kid with her trunk, catching him midair. The coordination and style of play by the circus-trained elephant impressed Billy, but not as much as her recklessness. He clapped as he ran closer.

"Billy!" James squealed. "You go next."

"I think not," Mary Louise said. "Billy is much too big for me to toss about."

"Am not. I haven't grown a hair in two years because of the potion."

"Even so, you are a sixteen-year-old human. You should be maturing and growing. Did you know elephant babies walk minutes after their birth? By that measure, I would say you are lagging."

"So what? I can float. Can a baby elephant float?"

"Take care with this young one," Mary Louise said. "He is delicate and not familiar with the dangers of the estate."

"But you just tossed him in the air like a toy? How is that being careful? Come on, James. I have a big day planned for us."

James squeezed Mary Louise's trunk. "Bye, Big Momma."

"Have a fun time," Mary Louise said, before turning to a visibly upset Leggy. "Do not blame me. You need to be more astute. I cannot find you every time the boy comes to play. He smells quite strong. Perhaps you should sniff the wind more often."

THE AFTERNOON SLIPPED by as Billy and James trudged across wild grazing lands. Billy, a hundred yards ahead, stopped as the boy doddled toward him. James chased every toad and snake that crossed his path. *We'll never reach the water hole at this rate.*

Kneeling to the boy, he grinned. "Quick, hop on my shoulders, and we'll have an ostrich race."

James bounced along Billy's back to his shoulders. Tucking his feet into Billy's armpits, James slapped him on the top of the head. "Run, ostrich, run!"

Billy took off like a rocket, swerving along the path and jumping off rocks, making the journey more dangerous than it needed to be. James never flinched. Instead, he encouraged Billy to hurdle downed trees and splash through small streams of water. Reaching the spot, James bounced off Billy.

"Follow me," Billy said, pushing the grass aside and pressing forward. Trickling water and the croaking of toads let him know they were close. A few steps farther, and the grass gave way to rocks and sand.

"Oh, geez!" James shouted. His eyes darted from the mountain of rocks to the rope swing hanging from a low branch. Crystal clear water swirled in the small pond. The cold water proved a lifesaver during the summer, but the chilly spring air could freeze a wet boy down to his bones.

"I found this watering hole when I first moved to the house. No one knows about it except for me." Billy tossed his shoes to the wild ferns and padded over the smoothed rocks toward the pond. He stuck his toes in the water and jerked them back out. "Yep, still freezing cold!"

"I wanna try," James said, stumbling as he tugged at his shoes.

"Let me help." Billy picked at the laces, freeing the boy's sweaty toes. "Moms always double knot. Once I couldn't get my shoes off for a week."

The boys stepped to the water, and James dipped his foot once, then again. "I like it."

"I dare you to rope swing into it."

James's callused hands grasped the tree's exposed roots, climbing to the surface of the small cliff. Kicking rocks off the side, he grabbed the coarse rope at the highest knot. "It's not moving?"

“Run and jump off the end. Don’t let go of the rope until you’re over the water.”

“Oh.” James stepped backward and examined the bumps along the cliff he’d have to avoid. His bare feet darted toward the water, and he jumped a small bump only to trip over the second, much larger one at the end of the root. A scream rolled from his lips as his arms shot outward. Head to back to feet, he bounced along the rocky edge and landed face first in the water.

“That was terrible!” Billy laughed, but the eerie silence caught his attention. “Oh, no!”

Billy staggered along the sloping cliff. He flipped James’s face from the water into the air. The boy took slow breaths but wasn’t moving. Tears welled in Billy’s eyes. “Help! Someone help!”

Tugging James onto his back, Billy concentrated on his ability to float into the air. The two boys lifted off the rocks, but the extra weight of James kept them floating only a few feet from the ground.

The shivering of James’s tiny body as the cold air met his water-soaked clothes kept hope alive he’d be okay. As they moved toward the field, Billy tugged at the blades with his free hand, propelling them through the tall grass. They moved fast, scaring the wild hogs foraging for bugs and roots.

Billy’s ears pounded as the image of James’s still body floating in the pond overtook his thoughts. *How could I be so stupid? James is hurt because of me. I hope George knows what to do.* The fence of the estate in the distance gave him hope of finding help. James moaned as he became conscious.

Grazing the jagged top of the fence, Billy laid James on the soft grass at the most northern edge of the Gardenia

Estate. He stared deep into James's eyes, praying for him to return to normal. "James?" He snapped his fingers near his nose. "Can you hear me?"

James's body shook as he stared at the grass for several minutes. His glossed-over eyes worried Billy. Rubbing the lump on the back of his head, James cried, "My head hurts!"

"I bet it does. Let me look at it." Billy parted the boy's hair, finding a lump the size of an orange, the really small ones that peel easily. "It's not too bad. No blood."

"I want to go home. I want my momma."

Billy dropped his head, glad the boy was feeling alright. He lifted James to his back and carried him across the estate to the cottage. Betsy opened the door, and her smile dropped like a rock in a pond. "What happened to you? You're all muddy and wet."

"We were playing, and James hit his head."

Betsy seized James and laid him on the couch, but he popped right back up. "Ouch!"

Without a word, Betsy rushed to the kitchen and returned with a cold dishcloth. She wiped his face and kissed all the newly cleaned spots.

"I guess I'll be going," Billy said. Neither James nor Betsy stopped him to ask questions or accuse him of putting James in harm's way. He willed himself invisible and slunk from the cottage door.

Billy shuffled along the dirt path to the henyard. He stepped up the small hill, and the white three-story henhouse greeted him. When he was younger, chasing the hens proved a good time. Now, with Myrt gone and James being hurt, the thought of such a childish pastime filled him with sorrow.

Sitting on the dirt, he watched the hens pecking at the

ground, not one bothering to squawk at him or try to attack. *Maybe Mary Louise is right. I need to mature. James could've died today because of me. If I'm going to be a big brother, I need to grow up. George will know what to do.*

Lumbering to the lab, Billy knocked on the door. Bruce the Loyal creaked and moaned as the handle clicked into the lock position. The rejection hit Billy hard, and he turned to leave, recoiling at George's sudden appearance in the doorway, his goggles tight around his thick black hair. "Billy. Are you lost?"

"No, sir. I need to fade my potion, like Myrt."

George yanked off his goggles and welcomed Billy into the lab. "Have a seat." He ushered Billy far from the ongoing experiment bubbling on the work desk. "What is this about fading? Are you feeling okay? Did more side effects flare up?"

"No, sir. I mean, I guess one did because I'm not growing any bigger. I'm sixteen, and I still look like a kid."

"People should have such problems. Have you been to the drug store lately? Aisles and aisles of chemical concoctions are designed to make adults appear younger. I'm working on a youth serum myself. A little extra money on the side, for my own old age."

Billy wandered to the cabinet where the potions were stored. Turning, he bumped into George, who nervously followed.

"This is what I mean. You don't even trust me in the lab when you're with me."

"It's not so much trust as—"

"I went to the henhouse and thought about the day Myrt

died. She grew so much older than she was, all because she drank a cup of tea."

"That was the potion fading and returning her to her physical age. Is this why you're here, to fade your potion so you can grow again?"

Billy lifted a bottle of birch wood and gave it a shake. "Mr. Kimall was here last week and delivered my copy of Boy's Life magazine. There was a picture of kids my age clearing the forest and building roads. They are proud. I want to be proud of something, and part of that is becoming a better brother to James."

George slumped back in the wooden chair, his eyes wide. "Spirits alive! You *are* growing up!"

"No, I'm not. That's the problem. I need to fade the potion and age like Myrt. I have to be seventeen, or at least look close to it, to join the CCC boys."

"You've had the ability the entire time I've known you. Go eat a cookie or drink a milkshake. The potion will fade, alright."

Billy slumped in the chair next to him. "Truth is, I'm afraid. What if I make a mistake and find I don't want to mature and be big? What if it's too hard?"

"Growing is always hard, but that's how you become a man. You make mistakes, and you learn from them and do better the next time. Fear will always be there, but you'll never regret being honest, hardworking, and trustworthy."

"I don't understand those things, but I guess you know this stuff. My mother always says you are the smartest person she knows."

"Does she now? Imagine that." George took a silver compass from the drawer. "I want you to have this."

“Your compass? I used to sneak in here and imagine I was a wilderness guide.”

“I know. It belongs to my father, and now it’s yours. You’ll need it more than me if you serve in the conservation corps.”

Billy started for the door, excited for his future. He turned back and hugged George. “Thank you.”

ERNEST WOKE EARLIER THAN USUAL AT THE SOUND OF footsteps in the lab. George's dress shoes clomped when he stepped, but these had more of a click tone and moved much faster. He threw on his specially made bathrobe and peeked out the glassless window of his house.

Betsy removed her heels and tiptoed through the room, opening cabinets and flipping pages of notebooks on the counter. Clearly, she was searching for something and didn't want to get caught. *She wants the invisibility potion.*

Though she'd lived on the estate for a few years, Ernest had noticed a change in her demeanor in the last few months. She'd taken to following George around the house and laughing at his stupid jokes. He knew when a fake romance became a means to an end, things never worked out rosy and cheerful.

Bruce the Loyal hissed and barked at the lab intruder, prompting Betsy to grab a notebook and shove it into her rather large purse. She opened the door a few inches to peek up the stairs.

Ernest glanced at his suit hanging in the closet but didn't have time to change. Running to the first floor of his house, he burst from the front door. Clutching the rope nailed to the shelf, he swung across the room, landing on the work desk.

His bare toes gripped the surface as he ran across the table and threw himself off the corner. A faint sound, like the flapping of a bug's wings, went unnoticed by the intruding resident. Ernest landed on the stone floor and grabbed the heel of her shoe, climbing her stockings to the hem of her dress.

Betsy gasped and stomped her feet at the sensation of a bug on her leg. She twisted her torso for a good look. Finding nothing, she looked about the room. "Ernest? Are you here?"

He kept his silence and jumped into her shoulder bag, landing on a tube of lipstick. Fumbling over pens and bundled tissues, he read the cover of the notebook. *The inventory pad? What would she want with this?*

She bounced up the stairs to the delivery door of the kitchen and out to the dew-covered grass. A bicycle near the door helped her speed to the estate's wrought-iron gate, where she hid it behind an azalea bush.

Ernest grabbed the seam of the purse and peeked over the leather. The street in front of the estate was a speedway as people headed to work. Without care, Betsy dashed into the traffic. Horns blared, and angry men shook their fists out their car windows. She dodged at least two cars before making it to the other side, her mind focused on other problems.

Ernest dropped back into the purse. The lining of the bag reeked of old, spilled perfume. The chemical scent pressured his eyes and blurred his vision. *Maybe I should've stayed home and minded my own business.*

Betsy's quick pace slowed. She seized a newspaper from a bench and tucked it under her arm. Nodding to gentlemen who tipped their hat and taking the time to gush over babies in buggies had her blending into the crowd without issue.

Ernest recognized the stone walls of the Great War Memorial Park, where the homeless sought shelter after dark. In the early morning hours, the place was paradise. Birds sang from the branches of fruit trees. Kids bounced on the see-saw, trying to drop their friends to the pit of sand under their seats.

A lone bench warmed in the full morning sun, far from the mothers huddled in the shade of a great oak. Betsy took a seat and opened the paper, reading from the back page to the front.

THE EARLY RISERS had come and gone, and the afternoon crowd clutched their brown lunch sacks, scrambling for benches. Ernest didn't have a watch, but the angle of the sun said it was half an hour before noon.

Betsy had read the paper several times, often peeking above the top as if waiting for someone. Maybe she was early, or they were late. Either way, Ernest had to use the restroom.

The closest public toilet was across the park, but it didn't matter. Entering such a place at his size left him open for being squashed underfoot. And he didn't want to think about the puddles that often formed on the cement flooring. The bushes would have to do for now.

Lobbing his leg over the top edge of the purse, he jumped to the bench and off the back slat into a pile of chewed sunflower seeds. The sticky shells clung to his cotton robe, and Ernest brushed them off as he neared the tree line.

Grasshoppers chewing on leaves stopped as Ernest pushed the stem of the plant to the side. Roaches burrowing into the tree bark didn't bother him, choosing to go about their business. Ernest cleared his bladder and headed back to the bench where a man stopped momentarily in front of Betsy. He wore a linen suit and white hat, and carried the notepad in his arm as he strode away.

Betsy folded the newspaper and dug in her purse for the lipstick. Ernest ran for the bench and jumped from a boulder to the wooden slat, grasping for the curl of her hair. Her legs wobbled until she reached the exit of the park where she walked fast enough not to draw attention to herself but still made good time.

Having made her way across the busy street and back to the mansion, Betsy paused at the delivery door, brushing her hair flat and arranging her dress. Ernest dropped from her head to her pocket.

James barreled around the corner of the house with Judy running close behind, her fingers stretched long. Their screams stopped as Judy scratched the hem of his shirt and yelled, "You're it!"

His feet gripped the rocks and he dashed to his mother in the doorway, ramming her in the leg. "Now you're it, Momma!"

"Oh, I'm gonna get you, you little rascal," she said.

Ernest bounced in the pocket as Betsy chased after the children. *Time to go.* With his robe tied closed, he jumped to the grass and hurried to the house under cover of pansies and bluebells. He climbed into the milk door and pushed the panel that opened to the kitchen. The riddle of Betsy's behavior hounded him as he traveled to the lab. *Is she some kind of spy or a doting mom? Maybe both.*

SOPHIE MAE YANKED OPEN HER CURTAINS AND SAT IN THE cushy seat of the desk chair. She leaned over the notebook and scribbled her thoughts. *A warm bed, nutritious food, family.* Such was her routine each morning, though she didn't understand why the task brought her such joy.

The grandfather clock in the foyer chimed ten times, alerting the household to the lateness of the hour. Tucking the journal into the desk's top drawer, she opened the square one on the left and pulled out the long bookkeeping notebook. Flipping through the pages, she made sure the information was up to date. She grabbed it and headed out the door to the library.

Mr. Kimall and George were already in the book-filled room, sitting in the wingback chairs near the enormous fireplace at the back of the library. Chatting about baseball, they laughed at the first base coach's behavior at the last game.

"He screamed so loud at the umpire his gum went flying," Mr. Kimall said. "Boy, it didn't take long for the players to get involved."

"I saw the picture on the front page of the newspaper," George added. "The headline said it took twenty minutes to clean the field after the fans threw their drinks and snacks in protest of the awful call." The dark tips of his hair peeked around the edge of the chair. "Miss Sophie Mae. Come in."

Both men stood as she crossed the floor and placed her notebook on the long study table. "Don't mind me. Continue with your conversation."

George sat back down and grabbed his own notebook, placing it on the table. "Ms. Catherine's been gone for a long time. I hope she's okay. Putting on such a fancy show could be dangerous with so many people out of work and hungry. They are angry the government is failing them."

"I almost forgot," Mr. Kimall said, lifting a newspaper from a crate holding several documents. "I have a niece that lives in California, and she mailed this to me."

Sophie Mae scanned the newspaper sprawled over the desk. The advertisements for sunscreen and beach toys were far different from Evenland, which boasted butcher shops and automotive repairs.

A photograph in the top left corner showed a couple standing in the sand, their clothing covering everything but their face and hands. Ocean waves crashed behind them. The headline stated they were royalty from Great Britain, hoping to strengthen the alliance between the two countries.

Near the bottom of the page was a much smaller photograph. Sophie Mae squinted at the image of a stage crammed with half a dozen people. Banners hung in the background, and the audience's blurry hands waved along the bottom edge, giving it a dreamy feel.

"That's her, right there," Mr. Kimall said, pointing to the image. "Catherine and her acting troupe are crossing the state and playing to audiences for donations."

George scanned the article, tapping his finger against the page. Suddenly, his eyes looked to Sophie Mae. "It says the troupe has raised $100,000 so far, and they are only halfway through the tour. Can you imagine what a sum of that kind could do here in Evenland?"

Mr. Kimall tipped the brim of his cowboy hat as he scratched his forehead. "I'm sure the actors will divide the money between their own cities. We might get a small part, but every bit helps."

Dink padded into the room and leaned over the table. "Did you start without me?"

"No," Sophie Mae said. "Look, it's Aunt Catherine."

Dink squinted at the photograph and shrugged. "She's so small. How can you tell it's her?"

"Oh, it's her, alright!" Mr. Kimall said, blushing the instant it slipped from his lips. "We, um, should get to business. I have deliveries to make."

George winked to Sophie Mae, who held back a giggle. Everyone in the house knew of Mr. Kimall's fondness for her Aunt Catherine and the awkward lengths he took to hide his feelings. *It's nice to have someone to love, no matter your age.*

Turning to Dink, George raised an eyebrow. "Did you forget your books?"

Dink lifted her left hand, and the notebook appeared. She laid it on the table and raised her hand once again, this time summoning a pencil and eraser. A satisfied grin spread from one cheek to the other.

"Let's begin." George opened his own book. "My most recent inspection of the fruit trees here on the estate show a slowdown in production. Well-fed trees produce less fruit. I suggest we stop watering them for a month and see what happens."

"That sounds like a great idea," Mr. Kimall said. "The number of people requesting food has grown. Even though most people have more money from work programs, there's an overall shortage of food to buy. Why, I read the government is paying the farmers to plow under their crops to stabilize the economy."

Dink straightened in her seat. "But there are so many hungry people."

"If the economy fails, there'll be many more hungry people," George said. "Dink, what have you learned from the city council meetings?"

Opening her notebook, Dink read over the notes she'd taken.

<u>*Monday, City Council*</u>

- *The city's emergency fund has dried up.*
- *Higher taxes on local businesses were suggested.*
- *Churches are encouraged to do more for the community.*

She slammed her notebook closed. "It's so irritating because the churches are also broke."

"I have the numbers from the soup kitchen," Sophie Mae said. "Sister Beth added ten more families to the Monday dinner and four to Wednesday. As food suppliers go out of business, she says they've had to rely on unscrupulous companies charging three times the normal cost for potatoes."

"Well," George said, standing from his chair, "I should return to work on the potion. It seems growing more food in a shorter amount of time is the answer."

"Are you talking about a growth potion?" Mr. Kimall asked. "We can't give people invisible fruit."

George furrowed his brow. "I'm getting close to a working formula. Betsy is helping me in the lab. She's a brilliant assistant, a talent which I'm sure she learned from her father, the botanist."

"I keep hearing that word," Dink said. "What's a botanist, anyway?"

"A person who studies plants."

"Oh. I guess that would help."

"Speaking of help, who's gonna help me load the truck?" Mr. Kimall asked, heading for the door.

Sophie Mae grabbed her notebook. "I will. Just let me put my book away."

"I'll handle that," Dink said, taking the notebook in her right hand. She snapped her left, and the book disappeared.

"How'd you do that?" George asked. "Did you discover a new side effect?"

"I've been testing my limits, and I'm learning what my side effect can do."

"Great!" Mr. Kimall said. "Then you can help with the crates. We'll be done in no time."

Dink slumped and followed him out the door.

Sophie Mae turned to George. "Do you think a growth potion will really help? This drought has been going strong for five years."

"We won't know until we try."

JAMES CROUCHED LOW IN THE GRASS LIKE A CHEETAH, WITH only his eyes above the blades' frayed tips. His fingers gripped the dirt, and his toes held the weight of his small body. With a single thrust of his legs, he pounced at Mary Louise.

ROARRR!

"Oh, heavens, an attacking tiger!" she played along. "A little assistance, Leggy."

The giraffe dropped the apple in her mouth and ran to James. In full retreat, the boy scrambled along the loose dirt, giggling and gasping for breath. His hair shot straight upward as he was lifted to the sky by the seat of his pants. Leggy's fruity breath covered the boy as she clutched his pant pocket with her teeth.

James stretched out his arms like airplane wings. "Faster! Faster!"

Galloping through the yard, Leggy jumped over bales of hay and watering troughs, circling back around to Mary Louise. Leggy released James to the elephant's dusty back and sprinted for the blueberry bush at the boundary of the property, her long, thin tongue dangling from her mouth.

James raised his hands and slid down her thick skin to the soft grass. Cuddling close to her head, he traced the veins in her huge ears. "They're like two giant leaves of a tree."

"I suppose they are," Mary Louise said. "But does a tree have such a versatile nose?"

Lifting her trunk high, it swooped to the boy's tummy, tickling him until he wriggled and screamed with laughter.

"I bet you were a good mother when you didn't have so many wrinkles," James said. "You always play with me even when you're busy, and you never get mad at me."

"How could anyone be angry at such an adorable face?"

"My mom, that's who. She's not being nice, and I escaped to visit you."

"Oh, I see."

James slumped his shoulders, flicking at the black ants frantically searching for the trail disturbed by Mary Louise's feet.

Mary Louise suspected Betsy was up to no good. Her dislike for the residents seeped from the cracks of her kind personality, giving way to impatience and ingratitude. Mary Louise understood this wasn't the time to pry into his family's personal affairs. "Would you like to hear another story, James?"

"Is it about the jungle?"

"In a way," Mary Louise said. "Long ago, a beautiful elephant lived in the jungle's forest. Each morning she turned up the dead leaves and branches, sniffing for the tastiest, most delectable roots. Always clinging tightly to her tail was a young calf watching and learning the ways of the elephant."

"Was that you as a baby?"

"Yes, James. The forest was my home. The trees towered over my head, and I felt as small as the praying mantis. One day, my mother and I searched for the sweet seeds growing on the far side of the forest. The journey took half a day and my hooves throbbed. I begged my mother to rest, and we lay under the low branch of a flowering tree."

James's eyes widened. "My mother never stops when my legs hurt. She yanks my ear to hurry me. One time it popped and hurt for days."

"Not all moments in life make for good memories, I am afraid to say," Mary Louise rubbed his hair. "On that day in the jungle, the crashing and grinding of trees grew closer. Mother hid me behind a bush and started into the woods to find the source of the commotion. All at once, her tall, proud frame crumpled to the ground, as if asleep. I brushed her ear, but she did not move."

James fell to his knees, and his arms stretched wide across her enormous stomach. His warm tears streamed through the channels of her wrinkles, changing her mind about the tone of her story. It needed a more uplifting ending.

"A group of men threw a rope around my neck and helped me up a ramp to a truck full of hay. Bananas and fruits were dropped inside the cage, and I ate a few, then fell asleep. When I woke, I was in a circus cart trekking the vast plains of the country."

"And that's where you met Mr. George, and he put a magic spell on you?"

"You are so clever," she smoothed his hair with her trunk.

"I'm sad you can't see your mother, but I'm happy you're here with me."

"Mothers are special creatures. Aggression and softness blend, giving them the ability to protect their young. The environment of a species is rarely hospitable, and the young must learn to navigate such obstacles."

"I guess my mom is like an elephant. She's always telling me to be careful and slow down. So…so that means I have two elephant moms!"

Mary Louise gushed at the thought. She'd always hoped to have a family of her own, but living in the circus didn't allow such relationships.

Rubbing his tiny hands across her hoof, his solemn expression lifted. "You need to tell Mom the jungle story, so she'll see that you can take care of me, and I can stay here when she moves."

"Why would she be moving?"

"At night, Mom thinks I've gone to bed, but I can hear her tapping the pen on the table. She's always staring at that old map. I bet the red X's are the towns that don't want us, and that's why we're still here."

Map? Red X's?

"I better get going," James said. "I'm supposed to be cleaning my room."

"Do not be too downhearted. I am certain we will be together for a long time."

James perked up, and his chest swelled. "You really think so?"

"Yes, now run along. Your *other* mother is probably worried."

Running for the cottage, he twisted back to Mary Louise. "You should tell Leggy about the jungle. They snatched her from her mother, too. I bet she'd feel better after your story, like me."

As James ran over the hill and out of sight, Mary Louise glanced at the tree line, searching for Leggy. Neither her fruity scent nor the galloping hooves carried on the wind. She shifted her weight and meandered through the field, calling for her friend. "Leggy?"

Mary Louise had known the giraffe since the early days at the circus, but that was the time before the potion. Understanding their place in the world took a back seat to eating and following the circus trainers' directions to avoid angering them. No such days existed at the Gardenia Estate. Food was unnecessary and the stress of life was banished to the past. But as the current drama with Betsy engulfed more estate residents, the long days lounging in the sun and interacting with the kind, coddling humans were slipping away.

First, George wants to let go of his performer's past, then Betsy shows aggression towards me. Now I learn Leggy has mother issues. It is becoming a circus around here.

BILLY GASPED AS HIS MOTHER'S STRONG ARMS COMPACTED HIS ribs. "Are you sure this is what you want?" she asked. "I won't love you any less, either way."

"Yes…" he struggled, pushing her off. "I won't do anything sitting around here as a kid any longer. Besides, my work in the CCC will help to stabilize the country and maybe even stop the drought."

"George was right. You've grown. Matured," Mrs. Worthington said, wiping her eyes. "I always knew this day would come. Your father would've been so proud."

"And I hope you'll be, too."

Billy took the muffin with a large top overflowing its

paper cup. Sugar sparkled over the golden surface like morning dew on the grass.

"It's funny," Billy said. "I've longed for sweets since the potion, but now I don't want it." Closing his eyes, he bit the edge of the treat. Dirt packed in the wrinkles of his forehead dislodged as he chewed. "It's so gritty."

He laid the muffin back on the plate, and the tingling started in his fingertips, then the core of his body. His arms grew longer, and his feet bigger.

Mrs. Worthington shuffled to the corner, unsure of what might happen. The door swung open, and George entered, joining her along the wall. She tucked her head to his chest, and his cotton shirt quickly absorbed her tears. "I can't watch. My poor little boy."

Billy clutched his throat as he hit his elbow on the edge of the coffee table. The ache of his stretching veins had him screaming in panic, but no sound escaped his lips. His toes and fingers sank into the rug under the table, and he curled into a ball. *I'm gonna be okay. I'm gonna be okay.*

Bolts of vibrant fabric streaked across the room as his vision blurred. The aching in his body had ceased, but he still felt sore, like all the times he'd fallen out of a tree. His vision darkened, and he passed out.

BILLY WOKE CROUCHED against the wall, draped in a thick blanket. He recognized the sewing machines of his mother's workroom. The light from the windows had turned dark, and his mother lay on the couch asleep. George sat next to her, flipping through a Modern Patterns magazine.

"How do you feel?" he whispered.

"Good," Billy's voice croaked. "I feel…very hungry."

George grinned. "That's good to hear. I left some clothes behind the screen there."

Billy wrapped himself in the blanket and stood with the help of the wall. His legs had the strength of gelatin. Exhausted, he fell into the plush chair behind the screen.

"You need plenty of rest," George said. "After that, a bath."

"You might be right—" Billy halted. His voice no longer high-pitched, but deep, like a man. "What's wrong with my voice?"

"Absolutely nothing," George said, pointing to the mirror. "It matches your new size. Look."

Billy moved toward the figure in the mirror at least two feet taller and seventy pounds heavier than his normal frame. He moved his arms. "Yep, that's me."

"Billy?" Mrs. Worthington called when she heard his voice. "Is that you?"

Quickly putting on the clothes, Billy stepped back into the room. Her hand covered her mouth, but her surprise was clear —surprise and relief.

"You feel okay?" she asked, checking his forehead for a fever. "Does anything hurt?"

"No. I'm tired and hungry."

"You need to rest. Go with George, and I'll cook you a nice warm dinner. Not too much, though. No need to be sick with your first meal." She cupped his cheeks. "Oh, my son. My adult son. I love you."

Billy dropped his arm over George's shoulders, and the two struggled down the hallway to Billy's room. "I know you're excited about being older, but you need to sleep. The potion takes a little longer to leave your body."

"I'll miss floating."

"I'm sure you'll find something better out there in the world."

A CELEBRATION WAS HELD in the kitchen two nights later. Decorative banners draped over the table, and a giant chocolate cake adorned the center. Mrs. Worthington and Billy stood side by side, greeting the members of the house as they entered.

"And who might this fine young man be?" Mr. Langston said, shaking Billy's hand. A smile cracked his face. "Good to see you maturing, Mr. Worthington. The world will be a better place for it."

Ms. Ruby grabbed Billy's hands and kissed them. "Praise the heavens! I'll have no more eggs in my shoes." She pinched his cheek and followed it with two pats.

Dink and Sophie Mae stared at the much taller version of Billy. "You're still my stinky little brother," Dink said, punching him in the arm.

Sophie Mae stayed behind as Dink headed for the table. "She's very thrilled for you. It's all she can talk about."

Billy didn't need to be told what he already knew, fairly certain she was watching his progress, hoping to follow in his footsteps. Mrs. Worthington tucked her arm under Billy's and led him to the table.

"What about James?" he asked.

"I don't know if they are coming. Betsy is still upset about James and the accident."

Knowing his part in James's ordeal made him nauseous. "I'll talk to them after dinner and apologize."

George outstretched his hands. "Ladies and gentlemen…" An audible sigh from the others had him grinning. "Just joking. We are all here to celebrate Billy's birthday—the last three, at least."

"I hope you brought gifts," Billy said.

"Honestly, we wish you the best."

Standing, Billy clasped his hands. "I've joined the CCC, and they have me stationed in southern Kansas, so I won't be too far. I'll miss all of you."

"Will you be able to write, assuming you know how?" Dink smirked.

"Cake time!" George shouted. "Billy and Sophie Mae can share the dessert."

Laughing and singing filled the kitchen, but other problems plagued Billy's mind. He needed to explain to James why he was leaving. Walking along the estate path, his legs moved quicker and more powerful than before. Every moment was fresh and an adventure in the making.

He stepped to the front door of the cottage and knocked. Betsy opened the door, shocked at his grown-up size. "Come in, please."

Sitting on the Mayville's old couch, he glanced around the time capsule room, with its Edwardian-style tables and stiff fabric chairs. Betsy kept the furniture as the Mayville's had arranged it, aside from the piles of toys and kid socks strewn across the floor. Either she didn't own anything, or she wasn't planning to stay long term. Billy didn't know which it was. After all, he'd only been an adult for a few days.

"The kids are in the bath," she said nervously. "Look, I'm sorry about being angry with you. I know you'd never hurt James."

"No, I wouldn't. But I am sorry."

"Oh, he's fine, really. He keeps talking about going to the pond. Boys want adventure, I guess." Betsy shifted in her seat. "So, you no longer have the potion in your system? How does that work?"

"I'm not exactly sure. When one of us eats or drinks, the potion fades. Sometimes we keep our side effects. Leggy eats everything and is still invisible."

"And George made this possible?"

"Why, yes. He's a clever man."

Wet toes pattered from the bedroom to the living room. The bottom half of James's pajama hung low and dripped water across the floor. "Billy!"

"Hiya, kid. How's the noggin?"

"How did you get so big? You're a giant, Billy! Can I be a giant, too?"

"I'm afraid not." He pulled James to the couch. "I have to leave in the morning, James, and I'll miss you a ton."

"I want to go with you."

"Not this time." Billy grabbed the Boy's Life magazine rolled in his back pocket. "See these boys? They are cutting trees and working in the forest to make life better for everyone. I'm going to join them."

"Will you be back in the morning?"

"No, but I should be home for Christmas, then we can build a fort in the big oak tree."

"Really?"

Billy hugged his honorary brother a final time. "Now, it's bedtime. Keep an eye on the calendar for Christmas."

Judy rushed into the living room, throwing a rolled sock at James. He chased her to the bedroom. Betsy hugged Billy. "Make sure you take care of yourself. The wilderness can be a dangerous place."

"Thank you. I wanted to leave this for James, so he remembers where I went." He passed the magazine to Betsy, who smiled.

"Oh, he's not likely to forget!"

DINK'S FEET limped over the edge of each step, her heart heavy. It'd been only three days since her little brother, Billy, faded his invisibility potion and left the estate to find his own way. She didn't think it a poor decision, but she'd hoped to be the first to go, the benefit of being the older sibling.

Plopping into the leather chair in the foyer, she threw her legs over the arm and dug for a handful of newspaper rubber bands from between the cushions. They were Billy's stash. Each morning he'd fire them off at her as she dashed to the kitchen. Wrapping one around the tip of her finger, she aimed it at the gold-framed paintings on the far wall.

The first shot missed the white daisy drawing. She reloaded her finger and switched targets to the abstract of the henhouse. "How could Billy leave me here alone?" She released the band, and it flew, hitting Sophie Mae in the face as she crossed to the kitchen.

"Oh, I'm so sorry," Dink said, rushing to the girl. "Did I hurt you?"

"It stings. I've had worse." Sophie Mae continued on her way. "What's this about being alone?"

"It's nothing."

"Billy had to leave sometime, Dink. Staying a kid forever only works in fairy tales."

Passing into the kitchen, Dink plopped to a counter stool and dropped her head to her hands. "He has annoyed me for so long, and I've dreamed of the day he'd leave; but now I'm not so sure he'll come back. I miss him."

"That's good to hear," Mrs. Worthington said as she entered the kitchen. Taking her white apron from the drawer, she laid it next to the basket of buttermilk biscuits. "I always knew you'd need each other one day."

Dink lifted her left hand, and a simple blue apron appeared, neatly folded. "If that were true, he'd have stayed."

"Don't worry too much," Sophie Mae said, hoisting the basket to her hip. "I'm sure Billy will return in no time, and you can go back to arguing."

Mrs. Worthington flinched at the roaring of Mr. Kimall's truck rattling the coffee cups on the shelf. "He's here, girls. Grab your things."

Dink slunk out the door. "Worst day ever."

"Morning, ladies," Mr. Kimall said. "Smells yummy in here."

"Have a sample," Sophie Mae said, tempting him with a basket of warm bread.

"Ah, no. Those are needed elsewhere." Opening the passenger side door, he yelled, "Move 'er out!"

Mr. Kimall and Mrs. Worthington stepped into the truck's

cab, and the girls jumped into the bed, backs against the cab. Two knocks and the engine bellowed to life. They shot down the road, and the ends of Dink's hair slapped her in the face.

Both girls waved to passing locals as they traveled to the Catholic church on the edge of town. Every Monday, Wednesday, and Friday, the church opened its doors for those in the community needing food and nourishment. For those seeking nourishment of the soul, the church was open seven days a week. Dink felt empty, but neither food nor religion would satisfy.

The truck swerved into the parking lot and stopped under the weeping willow near the church building's rear door. Mr. Kimall killed the engine, and everyone jumped to the gravel-covered ground.

A young nun barreled from the door. "Mr. Kimall," she squealed, giving him a big hug. "I haven't seen you in ages. How have you been?" The two of them walked into the building, delighted at the chance visit.

"Well, the supplies won't move themselves." Mrs. Worthington lifted the bread from the back of the truck, and the girls each grabbed a sack of fruit. "Best foot forward. Our neighbors need food, but also a big heaping of hope."

"Ugh," Dink said as her mother moved out of earshot. "A heaping of hope? How does she come up with this stuff?"

Sophie Mae tapped Dink on the shoulder, pointing to the sedan pulling in the parking lot. "Look over there. Is that Thomas's family?"

Dink dove behind the truck, peeking over the warm hood. "It *is* him. Why is he here of all places? His hair is so wavy, not greasy like he usually wears it. Do you think he is volunteering today?"

"Why don't you go ask him?"

"How is that even helpful?"

Sophie Mae strolled to the church's back door, but Dink stayed glued to the truck, her legs soft as bendy licorice sticks. The boy stepped closer to the building. *I can remain invisible until I get inside. When I'm near him, I can pull up my visibility. No problem.*

Heaving herself from the truck, the gravel slipped under her feet as she sprinted for the door. With her invisibility up, she yanked open the door and ran for the ladies' room. The group of women cutting fruit lifted their heads as the door slammed closed. "The wind is picking up," one said.

Mrs. Worthington, who'd been visible since leaving the house, closed the door until it clicked. "These things happen this time of year. The almanac calls for rain. Please excuse me."

Hurrying after Dink, she opened the bathroom door and locked it behind her. "Dink? Are you okay, honey?"

"Fine," came from the first stall.

"Why are you still invisible? We must communicate with the other volunteers."

"I thought we were supposed to hide from people," Dink's voice echoed off the stark walls. "You pulled me from school so no one would see I was different, but now it's okay?"

"We couldn't risk being seen before. They'd have taken George to jail when Ms. Catherine disappeared. People might still notice we're different, but we can't hide in the estate while others suffer."

Dink stepped from the stall and rinsed her hands in the sink. Mrs. Worthington stayed silent as Dink grabbed a towel to dry her hands. "What am I supposed to do when I'm recognized by the boy from school? I haven't grown in the last two years like my friends have."

"If he brings it up, change the subject. Mention how tall he's gotten or how much you miss being in class with him."

"Mom!"

"It works. He'll be happy you remember him and you think he is tall. Boys enjoy a good compliment now and again." Mrs. Worthington gave her a big hug. Dink squeezed her back, lessening the anxiety.

Dink peered out the cracked bathroom door listening to the mixed humming of the workers. She crept from the bathroom tugging her clothes straight, visible to all. The mothers and grandmothers waved as she passed the tables to the back where Sophie Mae divided the stalks of celery for others to chop.

"I'm glad you made it past the truck," Sophie Mae joked.

"Did you see Thomas?"

"Yes." Carrying a bowl of fruit to the fridge, Sophie Mae looked back and winked.

The doorway of the gymnasium proved great cover for Dink, who searched for the boy. Basketball hoops and loudspeakers hung from the rafters. Folding tables in neat rows hid the red and blue painted lines of the court.

"Where did he go?"

Sophie Mae leaned on the other side of the doorframe and pointed. "There."

Sitting at an outside table near the back was Thomas and his family. Dink's heart sank. "He's here because he's hungry?"

"Many of the families from town are here. We'll run out of seating if the jobs don't return."

"You've been talking to my mom again?"

"She's smart. You should listen to her sometimes," Sophie Mae said. "Why don't you bring him a bread your mother made. I'm positive he'll smile."

"Have you seen his smile? Perfection."

Dink took a roll from the tray and headed into the soup kitchen gym. Walking to his table proved more distressing than a spelling quiz. Standing next to his chair, she handed him the bread.

"My mother made these especially for this meal, and you should taste it before you leave and go back to your normal life and normal family." Sick to her stomach, she rushed for the kitchen, mumbling her wish to be invisible, knowing it was impossible with the gym full of people.

"Wait," Thomas called. "Thanks for the biscuit. I've had one, but two is even better."

"I'll tell her you said so." Dink turned, hoping for an escape to the kitchen.

"Are you that girl from my math class? That can't be right. Maybe you're her little sister?"

"No, it's me, Din—Lillian."

"Why do you still look the same?"

"Oh, you know us women—our face creams and vegetable diets. Anything for beauty." Rambling, she changed the subject. "You look taller. Are you taller? Geez, I miss having math with you, the smartest boy in class."

"I believe you were the genius. Mrs. Loundry made it a point to remark on your 'excellent' test scores every time she handed them back. A real teacher's pet."

"I don't remember," Dink lied. "It was years ago."

"I'm glad I came today. Usually, I have my sister bring food home for me. It's kinda embarrassing to eat here."

"You shouldn't be embarrassed—most people in town use this food as a supplement."

Thomas broke his gaze from Dink as his name echoed through the gym.

"My family is leaving. Maybe I'll see you on Wednesday?"

"If I don't have my invisibility up," she choked, as the words left her lips.

He laughed. "I never knew you were so funny. See you in a few days."

"Yeah. Bye."

Dink watched Thomas chase after his little brother. From the doorway of the kitchen, her cheeks ached at the intensity of her smile. She strolled through the tables, grabbing Sophie Mae. "You won't believe what happened!"

GEORGE SHIVERED IN THE LIGHT OF THE EARLY MORNING SUN as the delivery truck from Mort's Feed and Seed bounced down the Gardenia Estate drive. Glancing at his watch, he smiled. "Right on time, like always."

The truck was brand new, and its glittery paint sparkled in the sun, unlike the older models servicing most businesses. A mountain of square hay bales were piled on the bed and towered over the cab. Burlap covering the bales flapped at the corners, keeping loose hay from blowing off.

George rushed into the kitchen and raised his arms. "It's here. Are you ready?"

Sitting on a padded stool at the kitchen counter, Sophie Mae took another bite of her breakfast of warm oatmeal. The barn cleaning wasn't her first, but she humored the magician and paid close attention to how he wanted the task to be completed.

"The hay will be delivered to the barn. We'll have to move it inside."

"Just the two of us?"

"Most everyone will help today. Langston and Ms. Ruby will keep the kids busy until we're done. It's best to keep them away from the pitchforks." George dashed back outside to the delivery driver and patted him on the back.

"Morning, Mr. Cain. Ready for a fresh load?"

"All cleaned and raked. Drive around back, and I'll open the doors."

George raced into the kitchen once again. "Wake the others and send them to the barn. We need to settle the hay before noon."

"What happens at noon?" Sophie Mae asked, rinsing out her porcelain bowl in the sink.

"I have plans with Betsy." George flipped the collar of his new work shirt and bolted for the door. A shortcut across the grass had him at the drop spot before the delivery truck. As he swung the doors of the barn open, his new boots gripped the dirt. *These are going to work out great.*

Mary Louise stretched her legs and sashayed out of the barn, her trunk lifting to the sky. The usually fresh morning air carried a familiar scent from her past. Tanned leather typically worn by animal trainers, wafted from George's new work boots. "You have changed your attire, George."

"Do you like it?" he asked, showcasing his new style.

"Where are your black dress shoes and long tails? Have you finally left the circus?"

"How is that possible, with you and Leggy reminding me of the good old days? Inside, I'm still George the Great who thinks about magic and the theatrics of life. Outside, I'm a normal Joe, ready to move some hay."

"And what drove you to become George the Normal?"

Before he could match her wit, Betsy came from the path wearing a pair of overalls and a straw hat. George blushed as she waved.

"Oh, I see," Mary Louise said. "Might I offer you some sound advice?"

"Can I stop you?"

"Be mindful of those who do not appreciate your authenticity. Love does not demand change."

George waved her off and hurried toward Betsy, who stopped and waited for his approach. He bent and kissed the top of her hand. "Good morning."

"Is that what this is? I'm not usually awake this early," Betsy said, fastening the top button of George's sweater. "You need to keep warm in this chilly air."

Mary Louise huffed and turned from the entranced pair. "Come, Leggy. We should let them get to work before they become distracted."

Leggy galloped to George, dragging her tongue across his cheek and to his hair, making a swirl on top of his head. Turning, she bit down on Mary Louise's flapping tail and followed her to the field.

"She's right. Let's get started." George handed Betsy a pitchfork.

"Must we? I hoped we could spend time in the lab."

The chatter of teenagers grew as Sophie Mae and Dink walked toward the barn. Leaning close to each other, a whisper had them bursting with laughter. George held his pitchfork with both hands. *It's so good to see them bonding.*

ONE PITCHFORK of hay at a time had made a big dent in the job by mid-morning. Sophie Mae tossed the dried grass to the back of the barn, noticing Betsy leaning against the ladder, wrapping a blade of hay around her finger, staring at George.

"Farm work can be tough," Sophie Mae said, wiping sweat from her brow. "Is this your first time to move hay?"

"Yes. I grew up in the city."

"The only city I've ever been to is Evenland, but George says it's not a proper city, like New York."

"Has George been there?"

"I think so. He traveled a lot in the circus."

Betsy's bored expression gave way to a disgusted glare as Mrs. Worthington approached the barn. Carrying a pitcher of lemonade and several cups on a tray, she wore a contented smile. "Break time!"

Dink dropped her rake and sprinted past Sophie Mae to hug her mom. "Did you need help in the sewing room? I'm sure Georgie can manage for the rest of the day without me."

"Fat chance," George said, taking a glass.

Sophie Mae leaned against the barn watching as Dink tried to wriggle out of work. George hugged Mrs. Worthington around the shoulders as they clanked glasses and shouted cheers. Mrs. Worthington blushed.

Betsy cocked her head and shoved her hands in her pockets. "Janet and George must go back a long way."

"Mrs. Worthington and Mr. George have been friends for years, long before I got to the house at least."

"Is that so?" Betsy grimaced. "Well, not every street is paved with roses." Strutting toward George, she draped his shoulder. "What did I miss, darling George?"

"A glass of lemonade for you. It's the best in the county. Enough pulp to give it bite, enough sugar to sweeten life."

"No, thank you," Betsy sighed at the joke. "I'm more of an iced tea girl."

George sipped the last drop and raised his hands. "Back to work. We've two hours to finish."

"I'll have lunch ready for Sophie Mae and Betsy," Mrs. Worthington said.

"Oh, that's sweet of you," Betsy said, grabbing George's arm, "but we have plans for the afternoon. I guess that leaves you more time for sewing. Lucky you."

Sophie Mae held Mrs. Worthington's hand as Betsy and George strolled to the barn. "You do make the best lemonade."

"Thank you." She gathered the glasses on the tray and sulked away.

"Wait for me." Sophie Mae dropped her rake and ran after Mrs. Worthington. "I need to find my work hat. We can walk together."

Mrs. Worthington had a solemness about her that perplexed Sophie Mae. From what she knew, the business was going well, and she had several orders for aprons.

Silence followed the pair like a shadow as they neared the

house. Sophie Mae turned cheerfully to Mrs. Worthington. "Have you heard from Billy? Did he make it to the camp okay?"

"I'm sure he did, dear. Please excuse me." Her attempt at a smile failed as she disappeared through the delivery door.

Change had taken over the Gardenia Estate and sought to dampen Sophie Mae's spirits. Oscar D was deeply missed as he helped his grandson, Nathan, learn to farm. Billy was off maturing. Betsy was different, more aggressive, while Mrs. Worthington's light spirit withered. *Why can't things be normal?*

The hem of her pant leg caught on a thorn bush as she headed back to the barn to complete the day's work. Bending to free the cloth, she found Ernest standing on a rock. Sophie Mae knelt. "Hello, Mr. Wade."

"We need to talk. Lift me to your shoulder and act natural."

This day is getting weird. While Ernest always rejected help from the residents, today he climbed to her shoulder, talking as they sauntered along the path to the barn.

"Have you noticed anything unusual about Betsy?"

"What do you mean?"

"I don't have time for this," he scowled. "She's been stealing George's notebooks and giving them to a mysterious man in the park. She waits hours for him."

"I'd almost forgotten, with Billy leaving and all. Dink and I saw her in town at the hardware store. She met with a man, but in a mysterious way, like they were strangers."

"Just as I thought." Ernest strutted along her collar to the other shoulder. "She's trying to get information out of George, but what?"

A queasiness made Sophie Mae sit near the edge of the path. "What if the man and Betsy are trying to steal potions? Mr. George could get hurt."

"Yes, and she's doing her best to distract him. Between the two of us, we can figure out what she's doing and stop it before the fire spreads."

MARY LOUISE'S trunk curled to her back, and dust drifted to her giant body. Installed a few years ago, the sandpit had become her favorite spot, despite it giving her an unkempt look. George called the attraction an animal instinct, but she preferred to call it a lifestyle choice.

The chewing and slurping of fruit perked Mary Louise's ears. The grains of sand rolled down her back as she shook the extra dust from her head and started walking toward the front gate of the estate. *What could Leggy be doing so far from the field?*

Leggy kept a steady pace. Her urgency worried Mary Louise, who wasn't accustomed to running. With legs heavier than lead weights, her heart pumped hard within her chest. Finally, she spotted Leggy a few yards from the gate.

"Leggy, dear. Out for a morning jog?"

Nodding impatiently, she huffed at the question as she continued on her way.

"I know you are upset. James informed me about your mother. I am so sorry."

Leggy stopped. Her long neck drooped, and her head swayed side to side as she yanked the grass from the dirt.

"My mother and I lived in the forest and spent days

foraging for the sweetest berries and milkiest leaves. Humans took her from me when I was so very young. I was raised in the circus and given only what I needed to survive and perform tricks. A lonely lifestyle, indeed," Mary Louise said, closing in on the teary-eyed giraffe. "We are alike in this way. Tragedy and pain gave us the resilience to move beyond a season and continue forward. Since the potion has given me the ability to speak to people, I have learned they, too, have such pain. Blaming George for the loss of your mother is a fruitless endeavor."

Leggy peered at Mary Louise, and her angry eyes softened. Walking to her friend's side, they started for the barn in silence.

"Perhaps if George knew about your mother, he would help us find her. He did help me rescue Gus from the circus not too long ago."

A spark of hope twinkled in Leggy's eyes. With less trudging and more bounce in her step, she dropped her head to Mary Louise and swiped her tongue along the back of her flapping ears.

"I will talk to George the next time I have a moment alone with him. Betsy has been occupying his time as of late. Have you noticed?"

A deep and disturbing hum came from the giraffe. Mary Louise didn't know exactly what she was saying, only that it wasn't pleasant.

"Warning him of her intentions might be wise. If you took the potion, you could warn him with your own voice."

Mary Louise curved along the path to the barn and Leggy bumped her at times. The farther they traveled, the more the giraffe veered toward Mary Louise. The big red barn was in sight, and Mary Louise started to speed up, but so did Leggy.

Pressed tight against the barn, Mary Louise surrendered. "Fine. I will not mention the potion again. Is it so wrong to miss conversing with my best friend?"

The white of a baseball peeked from the tall weeds, and Leggy grabbed it with her mouth. Swinging her head, she tossed it to the field, and it rolled several yards. Mary Louise grinned widely, chasing after the toy.

HENS MURMURED in the background as George trekked the tall hill near the henhouse. Placing his gas lantern on a rock illuminated the thick grass where he stabilized the telescope. Twisting the focus ring on the end, George peered into the small eyepiece at the falling meteors shooting across the sky. Vibrations came from the earth, announcing the arrival of the large pachyderm.

"Good evening," Mary Louise said, emerging from the darkness. "Thank you for allowing me the freedom to roam this evening. The meteor showers should be quite exhilarating."

"I hope so. I've been preparing for months."

"Will Betsy be joining us?" Mary Louise asked as she lowered her body to sit. "I would think this event to be a favorite of hers."

"It might be, but I didn't tell her. She's very talkative, and astronomy is more about the silence of the universe and less about magical potions that grow plants incredibly fast."

"I see. She is working you night and day. Has she explained her intentions for the formula?"

"Only that her father was working on a similar project, and she wants to complete it for him." George lowered his notepad and tapped the pencil to his chin. "How someone can be so driven by another's goal is beyond me."

"Perhaps you should be cautious of those you hardly know."

"Betsy? We all know her. She's lived in the cottage for the last two years."

"Making her recent interest in your work even more suspicious."

George bent to the telescope, making notes every few seconds. Having put the conversation of Betsy out of his mind, he pointed to the sky with excitement. "Look, there! Spectacular, isn't it?"

Mary Louise followed the orange streak across the sky and returned her gaze back to George. "I have a matter of great importance to discuss with you."

"Does it have to be right now? The whole silence of the universe thing…"

"Of all the people, I trust you the most with another's emotional discontent."

George laid his notepad and pencil to the rock and joined Mary Louise in the grass. "Who is unhappy? Is it Betsy? Does she want to leave?"

"For star's sake," Mary Louise huffed. "Betsy is not the only show in town."

"Is it you?" He rubbed her ear and smirked. "You'll always be my favorite elephant, and I promise to never replace you."

Mary Louise blasted him with moist trunk air.

"What?"

"Stop messing about. I have a serious problem you must address. Leggy has tried to run away."

"What? Why?"

"Billy and James escorted her to the imagination room, and she remembered her mother."

"Oh, that explains the hoof prints on the stairs. Why would Billy take her there in the first place?"

"Does this behavior confuse you? Billy does what Billy does. If we cannot act, Leggy will leave the estate for good."

George lay back on the hill and stared past the stars to the dark sky behind them. *Circus owners take the young from their mothers to break the family bonds. Apparently, they're doing a terrible job. Mary Louise wanted to save Gus, and now Leggy wants her mother. This place will become a zoo before too long.*

"I suppose there are records concerning animal exchanges and sales," George said, "but viewing those records will require a little sneaking and acting."

"What an exciting prospect for you to undertake."

"Oh, you're coming with me. And Leggy too."

"How will we travel? Walking across the country is not a practical plan."

"I'll have to scrimp and save for a vehicle large enough to carry a goofy giraffe, an overly confident elephant, and a humble magician."

"Our very own traveling circus! When should we depart? I will need to pack a few hats and ribbons."

"Don't put the elephant before the marching band," George said. "Traveling will be hard with fuel stations closing and food options shrinking. It could take time with the economy worsening. Maybe a few years."

"I suppose you cannot help the timing. At first sunlight, I will bring the news to Leggy. It will thrill her."

"Yeah. Thrill."

SOPHIE MAE SKIPPED STEPS AS ERNEST CROUCHED ON THE TOP of her head, gripping the wavy strands of hair like reigns.

"Hurry, before they see us," Ernest said.

Sophie Mae weaved through the chairs and tables of the foyer, pushing the secret panel leading to the kitchen. The delivery door handle clicked, and she froze at the pitch of Betsy's voice from outside. "Oh, George, you're so funny!"

"Why is George falling for her lies!" Ernest yelled, swinging right as Sophie Mae darted for the stairs to the lab.

Tripping on the first step, Sophie Mae tumbled to the stone landing at the bottom. Pain shot from her ankle to her back as she hobbled to the door of the lab. Bruce opened immediately and they ran inside the room, closing the door behind them.

"Can you stall them?" she asked the door handle. "Give me time to hide?"

Bruce grunted. Sophie Mae didn't know what it meant as she had spent little time interacting with him. She hurried to the work desk and squeezed behind the stored cylinders of gas.

The door handle rattled as George tried to enter the room. After several minutes, Bruce let out a whistle, allowing the door to swing open.

"I'm not sure," George said to Betsy. "Sometimes, Bruce makes strange noises. He's harmless. Did you bring the marinated seeds we need?"

Betsy pulled a bottle from her purse. "I wouldn't forget the most important piece of the formula. My dad always kept a jar of them on the counter. He used every last seed. I was lucky to find these."

George took her hand and led her to the cabinet where he loaded her arms with beakers and vials. Arranging four glass jars in his hands, he followed her to the worktable. "We were really close yesterday. It helps that you write the details. You have such beautiful penmanship."

"I can't wait to test the potion. Can you imagine how great the garden is going to look when the roses are the size of elephant feet and the production of walnuts doubles?"

"Oscar's going to be impressed. I would've never thought to make a growth serum for plants. Why, it could give the average citizen the ability to grow mounds of food anywhere, in their yards with old tubs and toilets." George passed her the notebook. "Thank you for sharing the formula with me."

"Oh, I'm certain you would have thought it up, eventually. You're the smartest man I know."

George flicked on the Bunsen burner and turned to Betsy. "You're the best assistant."

Sophie Mae felt a scream curling from her lungs as Ernest tugged her roots, angry at the best assistant comment. She covered her mouth and used the other hand to pinch his clothes and lift him to the cobblestone floor, giving him a severe look.

Glass containers rattled as George struggled to keep up with the directions read aloud by Betsy. "Two drops of rosewood oil."

"We tried two yesterday," George said. "Are you sure about the amount?"

"Positive. Today we have the seeds, remember? Trust me."

Snake powder, wormwood, and a bit of chlorophyll rounded out the ingredients. George stirred them with a long, thin spoon. The thick, goopy mixture didn't bubble or hiss. "This can't be right," George said. "My concoctions always make some kind of sound and usually explode."

"Maybe because you're always doing it wrong, dear."

Sophie Mae clenched her fists at Betsy's mean words. *She won't get away with this. Mr. George deserves better.*

George examined the beaker of growth formula, holding it near the lightbulb hanging from the ceiling. "It's very plain. We should add color. Maybe green for the plants."

"It doesn't need anything." Betsy crossed the floor and

grabbed the wooden box of dirt from the sill and set it on the desk. She shoved her finger through the top layer of soil and dropped a single green bean seed into the hole. "It's your turn."

"Stand back a few steps," George warned. "You never know what's going to happen."

George bent his knees and secured his goggles. The beaker's pour spout rested on the side of the planter, and the potion spilled to the dirt. Both Betsy and George watched the concoction seep into the soil.

Sophie Mae peeked over the edge of the desk, bracing for the reaction. Several minutes passed, and nothing happened.

"Too bad," George said, taking the beaker to the cabinet, pouring the liquid into a bottle. "It doesn't always work the first time."

"Or the tenth, apparently," Betsy said under her breath.

Returning with the bottle and a marker, he handed them to Betsy. "Label it *Fail #10*."

Betsy placed the bottle on the desk. "This is frustrating."

"Magic takes time. We'll figure it out. There's no hurry, after all."

George moved to comfort her when the box of soil rocked on the desk. Standing away from the experimental potion was the right choice as the seed burst from the dirt and a stem with a tiny leaf grew. A few seconds rest, and it shot over three feet tall. The nails holding the box together popped from the wood, and dirt spilled across the desk.

Betsy kissed George on the cheek as the plant grew to the rafters and weaved itself around the beams. "You did it!"

George followed the plant's progress as it slunk along the

walls to the sunlight coming from the windows. "This will revolutionize the food industry. We did—"

He silenced as Betsy winked and snatched the bottle from the counter, shoving the formula into her bag. She darted for the doorway and ran up the stairs. George dashed after her but tripped on a vine spreading across the floor. Sitting on the ground, he rubbed his hair. "Well, that was unexpected."

Sophie Mae's chest panged. "Should we show ourselves and help him?" she whispered to Ernest.

"No. When he's upset, he likes to think through the problem in solitude. We'll talk to him later."

With a pair of trimming shears, George attacked the farthest end of the plant, clipping it into two-foot sections. The vine quickly filled the metal trash can where the pieces shriveled faster than an average plant. George carried the vials to the cabinet and locked the door. Dropping his white coat on the hook, he switched off the light and left the room.

LIFTING the small travel bag higher on her shoulder, Betsy stepped off the bus to the mat that read Welcome to Wisconsin. State flags attached to a tall pole bustled in the wind. With ample lighting and lemon-scented trash cans, the bus station was the cleanest she'd seen in nearly a decade.

Counting the squares along the concrete sidewalk was a trait she'd inherited from her father who worked long hours but always made time for her in the evenings. It wasn't until Brunhold joined in his research that his health took a turn for the worse. A year later, he was admitted to a state hospital, where treatment of the patients was questionable, even for the most prestigious in society.

Betsy didn't question her mother's decision to move him to the ward, as she wasn't known to make impulse decisions. Time marched on, but his mind remained locked in the past, far from those who loved him.

Standing outside the Wisconsin State Hospital, her feet were unwilling to take the next steps. She watched as nurses pushed wheelchairs from the side door of the two-story building. They didn't smile or engage the patients in their chairs, leaving them under an old willow tree as they returned inside to retrieve others. The patients stared straight ahead, blankness etched across their faces. *A mark left by an uncaring world.*

Betsy yanked her bag closer to her neckline and shook the thought from her mind. She strode through the front door and grimaced at the smell of antiseptic. An older woman in a white nursing hat staffed the information desk. "May I help you?"

"Yes. I'd like to see my father, Benjamin Miller."

The nurse flipped the pages of a book to her left. She ran her finger to the middle of the page until crossing a highlighted row. "Mr. Miller is in the mental ward. Go straight and make a right to the east wing, room 341."

"Thank you," Betsy said.

The cold, distant walls of the white corridors filled Betsy with dread as she padded to the east wing. She glanced at the lifeless people crowded into each room. Some peered out the windows to the old trees. Others stared at the doorway, stuck in a world they couldn't escape. Betsy held her stomach as the growing smell of alcohol and urine made her nauseous.

Brass plaques hung outside each doorway. 209 - 210 - 213 read the numbers as Betsy advanced down the hallway. Her body trembled as she thought about her father, unsure what to expect of the once great man's condition. He'd been a light for her path growing up, and she needed a little light right now.

Room 341.

Betsy took a deep breath and stepped into the room, surprised by the pleasant scent of lavender. A white curtain hung from the ceiling, dividing the space. Betsy looked at the man in the bed. It wasn't her dad. His nightstand held an overflowing bouquet of lavender blooms supporting a hand-drawn card with a stick figure man and a small child.

Reaching for the divider curtain, she peeked inside. Her father lay sleeping in the bed, covered by the standard white cotton blanket. A small, sunny window drew attention to framed photographs on a thin writing desk. They collected dust.

A yellowing photograph of her parents on their wedding day caught her attention. Her mom resembled a princess in a slim white dress with pearl buttons, her dad sporting an elegant dark suit. They posed on the steps of the church, both young and in love. Moving down the row, the image in the last frame broke her heart.

Another young bride, beautiful in her own right, posed on the same steps. She appeared to be alone, save for her right arm bent along the fold of the print. The black felt cardboard on the back dropped to the table as she gently tugged the picture from the brass frame. The corner of the image stuck to the glass and peeled off the inked layer of the paper.

Holding the picture in her hand, she bent the folded part

outward. Brunhold stood next to her, barely a smile on his face and deception buried deep within his sapphire eyes. "How could I have been so naïve?"

The rustling of stiff cotton sheets had her tucking the picture into her pocket.

"Well, hello there, pretty lady," Benjamin said. His skinny legs emerged from the covers and dangled off the side of the bed. Sores covered his ankles, but the man didn't seem bothered.

"I'm sorry. I didn't mean to wake you."

"Nonsense. Sleep is nothing compared to my beautiful bride's face."

There it is again. He doesn't recognize me and thinks I'm Mom.

"Dad, it's me, Betsy Ann. Don't you remember?"

"Now, don't trick me into trouble, Bertha. It's been a long day in the lab, and I'm not up to your games." He smiled and patted the bed. "Come closer. I'm afraid I've misplaced my glasses again."

Betsy sauntered to the small cabinet near the door. Next to the pitcher of water and a copy of Reader's Digest were his glasses. Sitting on the edge of the mattress, she handed him the spectacles. "After all this time, you still can't keep up with your glasses. How are you feeling?"

"Fine, dear. Better than fine. I think I'm on to something with the formula. I'm missing an ingredient that makes it stable."

"Did you try argan seeds?" Betsy offered.

"I have not. Argan seeds? Why didn't I think of that before? You really are a lifesaver, Bertha."

Speaking was tricky around her father. A single word

could transport him to another place in time, a memory within his trapped mind. Okay with being her mother for the moment, she kept a close eye on her dad, fearful of his violent outbursts, a side effect of his mental state.

"Say, did you talk to Betsy Ann today? I'm worried about our girl. Why she married that man, I'll never know. What man doesn't take to his own children?"

"Maybe she knows she made a mistake? That she was misled."

Benjamin leaned forward, handing her a secret picture from between the mattress and box spring as if hidden from the world. A young woman cradled a small baby wrapped in a striped blanket.

"What a smile the kid has," he said. "James is the spitting image of Betsy Ann for sure."

Barely recognizing herself in the photo, her eyes teared. "You kept her picture under the mattress all these years. She must've brought you shame."

"On the contrary, I keep it safe there. It's all we have left of Betsy since Brunhold stole her away."

Betsy paced the tiles in front of the window, biting the rough ends of her nails, unable to take the emotional strain. "I have to go. I want to spend more time with you, but I've made a mess of things. If I see Betsy, I'll tell her you said hello." She headed for the edge of the curtain, turning back as he spoke.

"Please tell her I miss her a great deal, and I want her to come home and bring the kids. We can take care of them and keep them safe and happy."

Without saying a word, she stepped behind the curtain and

to the door. The labored song of her father brushed past her ears.

Rosewood oil soothes the soul,
Striking in the dark…

If only we could be a family again. Goodbye, Dad.

DINK REACHED INTO THE CRISP HAY OF THE HEN'S NEST. HER fingers grazed the hard shell and grabbed the egg, adding it to the others in her basket. Noticing the blue, brown, and white eggs needed a good washing, she raised the handle to the bend in her elbow.

Fresh air greeted her as she stepped from the small henhouse. The gate surrounding the chicken coop slammed closed, and after a few steps toward the main house, she came upon James. He was lying on the grassy hill peering at the clouds passing overhead. A piece of straw flipped along his teeth, a habit he'd picked up from Billy.

Dink settled on the earth beside him. "What do you see?"

"Nothing."

"Well, that cloud looks like a leprechaun dancing on a rainbow."

James kept his eyes trained on the bright blue sky, holding steady behind the fast-moving clouds. His concentration kept him tight-lipped.

"Dessert has been a disaster for the last week. Sophie Mae tells me the muffins aren't sweet enough. I keep telling Mom to use more vanilla, but she—"

"Who cares about food?" James said, popping to his elbow. "My momma's been gone for days. She used to disappear at the train station but not this long."

"Sorry," Dink said. "Where might she have gone? Do you have a grandma or an aunt that would take her in?"

"We only have each other. That's what Momma says." He cradled his legs. "Why did she leave when we have food here? I guess I drove her crazy like she always said I would."

"Come with me." Dink held James's hand and the two of them walked the path to the house. James used his free hand to strip the leaves from the bushes growing wildly into the walkway.

"You know my mother is Mrs. Worthington?"

"Duh."

"Well, there used to be a Mr. Worthington, my dad. We lived together in a small house rented from a local businessman. My dad was strong and tall, and his voice carried like a sergeant in the army. He kept a strict schedule until the day he didn't wake for work. When mom was busy, I peeked into his room. He lay there, his entire face covered in red and white bumps. When I close my eyes at night, I can still smell the stench of the infection."

"Why are you telling me this?"

"The doctor said he caught the smallpox from working around others who had it. But I thought it was my fault after visiting my sick friend."

"You killed your own dad?"

"No. My friend got better. Most of the men at my dad's job died. That's how I know it wasn't my fault. In the same way, your mother didn't disappear because of you. Maybe she left because she thought it best for you and Judy."

"Like an elephant mom who leaves her baby to look for danger?"

"Sure," Dink said. "After my dad died, Mom became a different person. She sulked around the house and barely noticed me or Billy. We couldn't pay the rent and moved in with a friend in the Hooverville. Life became worse until Ms. Catherine offered us a home here on the estate."

"And it made your mom nicer?"

"It gave her time to relax, knowing Billy and I were going to be okay. Eventually, she remembered who she was and returned to her old self."

"So maybe my momma is finding her old self?"

"That's right. She needs space to work through the bad memories."

"What if my momma doesn't come back? What will happen to Judy and me? We prank the adults so much they probably hate us."

"No way. We adore the two of you. Don't forget, Billy treats you like a kid brother. We're a family now."

Dink felt the tension in his hand loosen as they passed the rose mound growing thick with weeds. Suddenly, James stopped and yanked Dink's arm. "What's that sound?"

"I don't hear anything," Dink said.

"It sounds like a prowling creature. A dirty, stinky, prowling rodent."

ARRGG!

Judy, with her tangled hair and attacking eyes, sprang from the firebush and ambushed James. Whirring in a circle, he grabbed at his sister clutching his shoulders. A deafening scream crossed his lips as she licked his cheek. "Gross, girl! Get off me!"

Judy landed on all fours and made a stink face at James before sprinting to the cottage.

"Come back here, you rotten sister!" James said, chasing after her.

With their voices trailing over the hill, Dink continued alone. Her thoughts turned back to her dad and the tragic end to his life. She drew her slumping shoulders back. *If my experience with losing Dad helps James, then something good came from it. That's what Mom would say, and she's usually right.*

The prickly legs of an insect scraped her ankle. Stomping her feet produced a faint squeak. Ernest ran across the cement slab, waving and smiling. She knelt to the tiny man. "Sorry, Mr. Ernest."

"Good afternoon, Ms. Dink," Ernest said. "I'm glad to see you. Crates are blocking the milk door, and I've been stuck out here for an hour."

Dink peered around the door. "I see. I'll move them after I put away the eggs."

Ernest hopped in the basket and rode it to the shelf in the pantry. Lifting the smallest egg took all his strength, as it was nearly as large as himself. "Don't worry about the crates. I need to consult with George on a more permanent solution. Maybe a tiny door within the door."

"Oh, like a mouse hole?"

Ernest ignored the comment and wrapped his arms around another egg. "I saw you with James. How is he doing without his mother?"

"Not so good. He thinks she went away because of him. Do you know where she went, Mr. Ernest? Did she leave because of the kids?"

"Best I can tell, Betsy is struggling with her past. Not only is she meeting with a strange man, but she's been stealing from George's laboratory."

"Stealing?"

"We need to gather more information, but I'm almost certain it has nothing to do with the kids. However, if she doesn't come back soon, we'll need to make a plan for James and Judy."

Dink nodded, heartbroken for the kids. She lifted the basket to her arm. "Can I give you a lift to the lab?"

"Thank you, but no. I plan to overcome my own hurdles. First, the outside door, then an elevator for the stairs."

Waving to Mr. Ernest, she stepped to the foyer of the home, her feet heavy on the stairs to the second floor. *Should I take a nap? Nope.*

The pounding of her feet stopped at the imagination room. With little thought, she opened the door and shuffled inside her old math class. The back wall of the room was made entirely of windows, ushering in a fresh breeze. The desks were perfectly aligned into five rows of six and occupied by her classmates who gazed at the teacher writing equations on the chalkboard.

Ducking into the last aisle, she took the empty seat behind Thomas. Being in a memory, he was the same age as Dink. She tapped the boy on the shoulder and he half turned. "You're late."

"Yeah. Hey, can I borrow a pencil?"

Mr. Langston jogged down the stairs and knocked on the laboratory door. The rattling of glass containers and rushed footsteps grew closer, and he straightened the lapels of his jacket. Glancing at his shoes, he spotted a fleck of dirt from the stairs. He flicked his handkerchief from his pocket and shined the black leather back to glory.

George tugged on the handle with a loose finger and kicked the door open. His hair stuck out on the sides, and his clothes hung disheveled. "Come in. You don't have to knock."

"I would prefer not to be surprised by your experiments. You have the list for me, Mr. Cain?"

"George, call me George. We live in the same house and

have the same friends." A notebook dangled from the shelf. George read over the opened page, ripped it from the spine, and handed it to the butler. "It's all there. I hope the new distributor has the sense to be more careful when delivering the chemicals."

"As do I. The previous company was operated by a car salesman who had no business selling hazardous chemicals."

"I wonder if his hair grew back since the explosion?" George grimaced.

"Might you have a moment for a personal request?"

"I might. What's on your mind?"

"I nor the others in the estate have seen Mrs. Betsy for a few days."

"Well," George said, putting a small torch on the work table, "Betsy stole the growth formula we'd been working on for the last few months. I'm not sure where she took it, but I'm fairly certain she's not using it to grow houseplants."

"What about the children? Will she come back for them?"

"I haven't the slightest idea what she plans to do. As for the kids, others in the house are taking shifts to care for them. I want to take care of them full time, but my focus needs to be on finding Betsy. The house is still at risk if the potion is found out."

"I understand. Will there be anything else?"

"No, and thank you, Henry, for helping me with the chemicals."

"My pleasure, sir."

Mr. Langston folded the list and stuffed it into his jacket pocket as he entered the kitchen, nodding politely to Mrs. Worthington. Flour covered her apron after making a fresh batch of banana muffins for the Hooverville delivery run.

Passing through the secret door to the foyer, the comforting singing voice of Ms. Ruby came from the sitting room. He paused at the doorway and watched her dust the frames on the fireplace. Though he'd always found her interesting, her new optimistic outlook drew his attention.

"Henry. Good morning."

"Can I speak with you?" Placing his hand on her back, he led her to the red velvet sofa. "I've spoken with Mr. Cain. He tells me Betsy has stolen his plant-growing formula. Her return is doubtful. James and Judy are being cared for on a rotation of estate residents."

"This is not good." Ruby perched on the end of the cushion. "Kids need stability, not babysitters."

"I agree. You've always said you wanted to have kids. We could raise them as our own."

"Are you joking? Raise kids at my age?"

"We will take on the task together. Life as a butler can be challenging. The children will ease the burden."

Ruby shot from the couch to the fireplace, rearranging the frames for a second time. "Well, don't think I'll be your wife. I can raise kids without the added hassle."

"I wouldn't think of it. We can add on to the cottage and have our own rooms. This way, the children aren't disrupted by moving. If Betsy should return, she will be thankful for the extra space. We can resume our normal lives."

"You've really thought this through. You're an amazing man, Henry Langston."

"I like to think so. Will you take on this adventure with me?"

"Do you promise not to stick me with the youngsters for days on end?"

"Yes."

"Do you promise to help me clean the cottage from time to time?"

"Yes."

"Will you rub my feet after a long day?"

"No."

"Well," Ruby said, "then you must not be serious about the 'adventure.'"

"Rubbing your feet requires a certificate of marriage, which we have declared off the table."

"Right, again. I'll move into the cottage—for the children."

Henry rose and took her hand. "Come with me. We must tell Mr. Cain right away before some one else steals the honor."

WALKING to the cottage proved challenging with Sophie Mae's sore ankle, but it was the highlight of her day. Pebbles crushed underfoot, and the blending of fragrances from the garden blooms always lifted her spirits. And if they ever needed lifting, now was the time.

Nearly a week since Mr. Langston and Ms. Ruby took over the care of the kids, Sophie Mae stood on the new doormat and knocked, holding a glass dish covered with a cheesecloth. The stomping of tiny footsteps ceased as the door swung open and hit the wall. James stood in his undershorts, a sock tied around his brow, with a stick raised above his head as he made a gargling noise, and ran off to the back room.

Sitting on the floor with a pink ribbon tied around his hands was Mr. Langston. "Miss Sophie. Welcome."

Ms. Ruby rushed in from the kitchen, wiping her hands on a towel. "Do you have the pudding? Please say you have the pudding." Sophie Mae passed it to her waiting hands. "Thank you, dear."

"How are the kids doing?" Sophie Mae asked the captive Mr. Langston.

"I've not spent much time with small children. They are quite fascinating creatures. Take this knot, for example. It is tight and slip proof. How does a child learn such skills?"

Sophie Mae let out a giggle that became a hearty laugh. Mr. Langston fought the urge, but the last few days with the kids had softened his stern nature. A boisterous chuckle burst from his lips as Sophie Mae knelt and untied the ribbon.

"What's the problem?" Ms. Ruby asked, returning to the living room. "Are you crying or laughing?"

"No," Mr. Langston said, straight-faced. Cracks streaked across his forehead as another laugh burst from his mouth.

"Heavens to stars! They've broken you." Ms. Ruby threw her fists to her hips. "Bath time!" Feet scrambled across the floor. She grimaced as water splashed from the bathroom.

Dink strolled through the front door, not bothering to knock. "It's like a jungle in here."

"Are you here to help, then?" Ms. Ruby asked.

"Um, no. I'm here for Sophie Mae. Everyone's ready for the meeting."

"I'll be back soon," Sophie Mae said. "Then you two can have a break."

"No hurry," Mr. Langston said. "It is all under control."

The girls walked from the cottage with bright light from

the windows shining on the dim path. Dink plucked a blue flower from an overgrown bush. "Why did we wait so long to have a meeting? It's been nearly two weeks since she ran off. She could be halfway to Texas by now."

"Ernest has been following up on some leads. He wanted evidence to give to George, in case he still thinks Betsy is innocent."

Shouting escaped from inside the room as the girls stepped under the dome light of the delivery door. Sophie Mae burst into the kitchen, and the bickering stopped. Ernest paced on the tabletop, kicking granules of salt while George darted to the stacked ovens and shoved his hands in his pockets.

Mrs. Worthington stood. "I'm so glad you two are here. We need a little calm."

Sophie Mae had always considered Mrs. Worthington the source of calm among the residents. Managing the household and the food distribution, she loved everyone, and they loved her back. But times were changing, and her spirit suffered.

Ernest outstretched his arms as he marched along the center of the table. "I told him you saw Betsy with another man, and he tried to squash me, like a common insect."

"Okay," Sophie Mae said. "We should sit and talk like adults."

George sat across from Mrs. Worthington, next to Dink.

Sophie Mae clasped her hands on the table. "Betsy was a wonderful mother and never said an ill word to any of us, but I believe she has changed. Dink, what do you know about Betsy?"

"I saw her talking with a man downtown. When I tried to follow him, he told me he knew about the potion and the house."

"That's not all," Ernest said. "I followed her to the park where she met a man, who I suspect was the same person. She goes to the park several nights a week to pass him notebooks from the lab." He lowered his eyes. "I called around asking about her. She never had a job. Where she went every day is a mystery."

"Is this the best information you have? That she sneaks around?" George rose from the table and walked to the food pantry. "I know you're all worried about my connection with Betsy. Even I was surprised when she took an interest in me months ago. If the circus has taught me anything, it's that not all doves are performers."

"Get to the point," Ernest balked. "Do you have better information?"

"From the first day she waltzed into the lab, I realized her attention wasn't genuine. I went along with it. Thought it'd be the best way to figure it out. She pressured me day and night for the location of my formulas and information to help her make her own." Strolling from the food pantry, he tossed a well-used notebook to the table.

Ernest's eyes grew wide. "The notebook with the formulas. You hid it in the pantry?"

"I did. It was easy to see she'd been snooping around in the lab, so I put out fake notebooks for her to take. Several nights I followed her to the park."

"I knew she was evil," Dink said.

"Maybe not evil, but possibly misguided," George said. "Some people feel they have to earn their parents' love no matter the cost."

"So, what do we do next?" Sophie Mae asked. "I mean,

she has the potion, and without proper testing, it could poison the entire food supply."

"Not to worry." George pulled a bottle from his pocket. "I switched the potions before she left. I gave her a burping potion that shouldn't affect plants in the least."

"All this time, you knew?" Mrs. Worthington asked. "Is that why you've changed who you are? To catch her in the act?"

"Mostly, but these sweaters and pants you made for me are very comfortable. I enjoy wearing them. Why would I change who I am for someone else? Even an elephant knows better."

Mrs. Worthington smiled for the first time in weeks. Her posture corrected, and Sophie Mae caught the familiar glimmer of peace in her eyes.

"We all know how clever you are, George, but we still have a problem," Ernest said. "Betsy and the mysterious man know about the magic. If they tell other people, the locals will flood to the estate for the potion."

"And don't forget about James and Judy," Mrs. Worthington said.

Sophie Mae stood from the table. "We have to find Betsy for the estate and the kids. Any ideas?"

SOPHIE MAE CARRIED THE CRATE FROM THE BACK OF THE field, taking in the morning sunshine warming her face. Dropping the bunch of oranges near the delivery door, she turned to George who sat near the maze.

"Do you think this will be enough?" Sophie Mae asked. "It's less than we normally bring but plenty for an early morning picking."

"It'll be enough. We just need to give the impression everything is business as usual. If a stranger is lurking around for Betsy, this will be the best way to spot him."

"What if people ask about our early visit?" Sophie Mae asked, leaning against the hedge wall of the maze. The branches shot out in all directions, taking advantage of Oscar D's absence.

"We say that we are going to miss our Saturday delivery and we're making up for it now." George bent to tie his work boot. "It's not like they think we're the bad guys, and they have to keep a close eye on us."

Sophie Mae admired George's new work boots—the sturdy kind with quick-tie notches. A simple tug of the laces upward tightens the entire boot.

"Are you done with your circus clothes? I couldn't help but notice you haven't been wearing them."

"Do you think I should store them, just in case? I think these clothes fit fine, and they're not as itchy. Mrs. Worthington made them. She's very talented."

Dirt billowed from the drive as Mr. Kimall's truck raced for the house. Braking several yards away, he spun the tires and faced the vehicle to the street. "Morning," he waved from the window.

George carried two crates and slipped them into the bed of the truck. "Sorry for the day change. I know it upsets your schedule, and the people depend on your deliveries."

"They do, they do. But don't discount their ability to adapt. Say, how's Billy doing in the corps?"

Sophie Mae slid her crate next to George's. "We haven't heard from him yet. I'm sure he's busy, and I hear the mail only runs once a week."

"That's all we have today," George said, latching the chains of the tailgate.

"Let's get a move on," Mr. Kimall cheered.

THE ENGINE CHOKED as Mr. Kimall waved to the kids in ragged clothes running along the village's outer wall playing freeze tag. Sophie Mae stepped from the parked truck, picked up a crate, and walked to a 'frozen' kid whose arms and legs were stuck in a falling position. She placed an orange on her stomach, which 'defrosted' her body. "Look, you guys!" she yelled to the others.

"I'll catch up with you in an hour or so," Mr. Kimall called out.

"Thank you," George said.

After half an hour of passing out fruits and asking the villagers if they'd seen a stranger, the no's piled up. Sophie Mae worried they might not find the pointy-nosed man from the hardware store. Facing the warm sunlight, she sat on a log next to George, who tossed an apple between his hands.

"Does it ever bother you?" Sophie Mae asked. "Betsy using you, I mean."

George squinted at the sun. "When you're my age, you expect such things. But to answer your question, yes, it bothers me. From the time I was born, people have written off my talent. It was nice to have Betsy around. She was very interested in my knowledge, and that doesn't happen often. Might never happen again."

"I wouldn't be too sure. I mean, Mrs. Worthington put a lot of time into fitting those clothes for you."

"Isn't that her occupation?"

Sophie Mae searched his eyes for sarcasm but only found confusion about her statement.

"Excuse me," a middle-aged man said. "Do you have any food left for my daughter?"

"Here you go," George flicked him the apple.

"Are you searching for that odd man? I'm new here but I think I've seen him just this morning. That's his car parked over yonder."

"Where did you see him?" George said, jumping to his feet.

"You aren't with the police, are you? Because living in this hole doesn't make us criminals."

"No," Sophie Mae said. "We're looking for a lost mother, a friend of ours."

The villager scanned for eavesdroppers. "He's been hiding out in the train station. When he's hungry, he tries to con us out of our food, but none of us are helping him."

"What does he look like?"

"Tall, thin. He has a long nose and chin. Very distinct."

Sophie Mae handed him the crate, still half full of oranges. "For your family. Thank you, sir, for helping us out. We make our regular stops on Saturday mornings, and I'll make sure I find you."

Tears welled in his eyes. "God bless."

George shook the man's hand before he left to surprise his daughter with the sweet fruits. Suddenly, George dashed for the train station, and Sophie Mae jogged to keep up. "What's our plan?"

"Don't have one."

"We can't just drag the guy out of the train station."

George stopped. "We don't know who he is or what he wants with Betsy. We don't know if they plan to tell others about the magic, and we don't know if he has others helping him. Where would our plan start?"

"You have a point."

Making fast work of the enormous steps to the train

station, the two of them passed through the rotating door. The musty odor had George covering his nose. “What *is* that?”

“Poverty,” Sophie Mae said. “The pay phones are over there.”

Sophie Mae led George to the northwest corner of the building. Few people occupied the waiting room, making the search for the sharp-nosed man easier but also leaving them more vulnerable.

A small corridor with dingy tiled walls looked promising to George. Signs hung from the ceiling and highlighted the location of the telephones and the restrooms. The telephone booths were built into the wall, and behind each door was a table and a single chair. George peeked through each of the frosted glass windows. Empty. A sign directed him to the men’s room where a piece of paper stuck to the door read ‘out of order.’ It was locked.

Sophie Mae plopped onto the bench near the end of the hallway. “This is a lost cause.”

“We’ve only begun looking,” George said. “This station was built long before I was born. It has secret areas the public never sees—an illusion of simplicity, like a magic trick.”

“But what are we looking for, exactly? I mean, we don’t even know his name. What if we pick the wrong pointy-nosed man?”

George ignored her question, wandering from the bench and down the hallway. Like a beagle on the hunt, he wandered left and right, searching the doorways before stopping in his tracks. “Do you smell it? Betsy’s perfume. Follow me.”

Taking a deep sniff of the air left Sophie Mae dizzy as the odor of rotten food and dirty people affected her. Aunt

Catherine said it was a psychological reaction, post-traumatic stress, from struggling in the dust bowl.

A half wall, meant to blend in with the station's décor, hid a door with a brass nameplate that read Electrical. George pushed it open and reached for the switches usually found near the frame. Three light bulbs flickered down a long corridor. "She's here. Very close."

"What should we do?" Sophie Mae asked. "I can ask the ticket clerk for help. Maybe the guards outside will protect us."

"No, they'll see us lurking around and think we're the problem." He flicked on a flashlight from his pocket. "Let's make ourselves at home."

SINCE LEAVING THE GARDENIA ESTATE, Betsy had lost track of time. Had it been a few days or a week? Such information seemed useless as she clasped her hands tight at the waist and paced the maintenance room of the train station. Her gut told her to run. Run back to the cottage, grab the kids, and hide far from this place.

Betsy wanted to believe she was a victim of Brunhold, but the truth of her motivations was crueler. Every decision to this point was hers. Feigning her interest in George for the potion and using the others' goodwill were but a few.

The logical inner voice that pushed her to the right choices in life failed after meeting Brunhold as a teenager. Since that day, the voice faded into silence. Brunhold appeared to be made from the same mold as her father. Smart, with a keen interest in science, she felt comfortable with him, despite him asking her to steal her father's research notes.

Standing in the dank room of water heaters and gurgling pipes, she owned her recent decision to stay with Brunhold—but this time, to stop him. Going back for James and Judy only put them at greater risk. His mind was a dark place, and his intentions selfish.

Brunhold bent over a dusty makeshift desk, whispering to himself as he scoured the books taken from the lab. Betsy flinched as Brunhold screeched the metal chair from the desk covered in scribbled notes. "The formula's not here. I'm not testing the potion until I see the formula."

"It works. Why don't you believe me?"

"It's not *you* that I don't trust," Brunhold said, inching toward her. He caressed her cheek. "It's the chemist. Men of science can spot a con artist when they're being conned."

"You wanted the potion, and I've brought it. We can finally leave the kids and take the first ship back to your homeland and complete the mission. It's what you've always wanted."

He returned to the desk, closing and stacking the books. Betsy considered how to put an end to his dangerous mission. Stronger and more cunning, he'd quickly stop her physical attack. Instead, she warmed to him, hoping to appeal to his heart.

"All those long days in the train station, I dreamed of us being together once again. I realized you were right about those kids. They ate most of my food and required too much of my time." Arms draped around his neck, her stomach lurched at the closeness of his breath. "Now we are together, we can return greatness to your people."

Brunhold looked deep into her eyes. "I'm afraid I've made a mistake. I thought you as smart as your father, someone who could help me, but now I see the truth. Yes, you're no longer needed." He returned to the desk to gather his things.

The muscles in her body tightened as she realized she'd wasted her life on the man. Spotting a metal pole in the corner, she snatched it and rushed toward him. "Your mission is over."

Brunhold turned, flashing his smug expression.

Adrenaline raced through her veins. He'd gone too far. Holding the pole at knee level, she swung it upward at his face. Brunhold attempted to duck, but the metal bar slammed into his right ear. His shocked expression faded as he dropped first to his knees, then to his stomach, unconscious.

Betsy kicked him in the side before taking the pistol from his jacket. "That's for threatening my kids."

Taking the potion and the books from the table, the footsteps outside the door gave her pause. She padded to the doorway and peeked into the dismal hallway. The rays of a small flashlight moved along the wall toward her. It had to be George lurking in the corridor. He was certainly intelligent enough to find her. The soft steps of Sophie Mae behind him refueled her anger.

Why would he bring her to confront me? She's innocent. He's no better than Brunhold, hiding behind a woman.

THE BRICKS LINING THE CORRIDOR WALLS DIDN'T MATCH THE near-perfect exterior of the train station. Stacked haphazardly, the rough surfaces of the bricks hinted at a quick construction. Rows of pipes ran the length of the walls and moaned and creaked their displeasure at having company.

Sophie Mae huddled behind George as his flashlight discovered cobwebs and enormous rats, adding to the haunted feel of the service area. She half expected to see a skeleton jut out from the wall, which would send her running for the light of day.

A few yards farther and they'd be enveloped by the growing dust in the corridor. The closer they walked, the slower George trudged, not sure what might be ahead. A human figure moved toward them with quick and confident steps echoing off the walls. It stopped at the edge of the choking cloud. Standing tall and defiant, Betsy held the stolen bottle near her head. "Did you come for this?"

"Why steal the potion?" George asked. "I'd have given it to you. You're better than this."

"You don't know a thing about me. I didn't exist until that girl fished me from a trash pile. The reality is people like me never really leave the garbage behind."

Sophie Mae's voice trembled down the corridor. "I wanted to help you. You had no home, and the kids were starving."

"What did you do with them?" Betsy asked.

"They're at the estate with Ms. Ruby. Come back with us. They need you."

"They never needed me—I *needed them*. I left them with you so they'd be safe and well-fed. Isn't that why you stay, Sophie? Why take a risk and move forward with your own life?"

George shined the light in Betsy's eyes. "That's enough. If you want to stay, stay. But I've got terrible news for you."

"This should be good. Go ahead, dear."

"The potion is a fake."

"I was there. I saw what it did. It's real."

"You're right, the potion we made did work, but I switched the bottles in the lab. Sorry."

Betsy's gaze shot left, distracted by a shadow in the cross corridor. She reached into the pocket of her dress, lifting the small pistol to eye level. "Never threaten my children."

The tall, sharp-nosed man emerged from the shadows and rushed toward her without fear. Her head jerked as he grabbed her hair. The gun fired too far to the right. The bullet ripped a hole through a pipe in the wall and sent steam plumes into the hallway. He stared at George as he threw her to the wall, her limp body slumped to the floor. Blood dripped along her nose.

"She was becoming a bother." He wiped his hands on a handkerchief. "George, I presume. Betsy raved about your brilliance with chemicals. Sadly, she isn't a good judge of such things. Not as smart as her father."

George's flashlight shined on Betsy, lying on the floor lifeless. He returned his focus on the man. "You know my name. It's only fair I know yours."

"She didn't mention me? I'm Brunhold, her husband. For the sake of time, please hand over the potion and formula."

Sophie Mae was stumped by the request as Betsy had stolen both at the same time. *Maybe she didn't give it to him?*

"What makes you think I'd have it on me?" George asked.

"Because you want a confrontation. Spending your days in a basement laboratory has to be boring for a circus magician after the lights and drama of the big top."

"What do you want with a magical growth formula?" Sophie Mae asked. "Didn't your dad teach you how to grow food the proper way?"

"You want to know my plan? Maybe I should tell you, so your part in my success will be forever etched in your mind." Brunhold's smug expression held as George became invisible. "Another circus trick? Oh, well." He picked up the pipe and started toward Sophie Mae. "Maybe you'd be so kind as to produce the potion."

Sophie Mae kept her eyes trained on Brunhold, refusing to look for George and give away his location. With only a few yards between them, she recoiled at the emptiness behind Brunhold's bright blue eyes.

A lightbulb flickered in the corridor. She dropped and covered her head, each gasp heavy on her chest. Brunhold stumbled toward her, falling to the dirt. Sophie Mae glanced at George holding him by the heel.

"Run!" George said.

Brunhold recovered and swung at the space behind him, spinning in place as the metal cut through the air. Another swing and the pipe stopped, hitting the invisible George in the stomach. Brunhold shook him off the pipe, and George's limp body trickled to the ground like oats from a torn bag.

"Magic is a poor replacement for strength and cunning."

Sophie Mae raced for the entrance, feeling the vibrations of the undeterred man's feet along the dirt. Turning to look back, she ducked as the pipe swung for her head. Panic seized her. She crouched to the ground as Brunhold hobbled toward her with a devilish smile.

Suddenly, Brunhold's torso shot backward. Spit and blood sprayed from his mouth. The heels of his shoes scraped along the dirt floor as he slammed into the back wall. A thud echoed like thunder in the tunnel. Bricks tumbled from the wall, covering his arms and legs.

The corridor grew quiet. Sophie Mae lifted her head enough to search for George. Her chest tightened at the sight of Brunhold sprawled on the floor, blood pouring from his head. *I must be hallucinating.*

Dust billowed from the bricks on the ground. Her breathing stifled as she willed her legs to run from the tunnel. The hallway seemed to grow longer the faster she ran. A muffled and painful voice boomed in her ears. Something gripped her right arm, and the fist of her left swung but stopped at the man's face. "Mr. Kimall?"

"It's only me," he said, holding her shoulders. "Are you hurt, little miss?"

"What just happened?" Sophie Mae asked. "Where did you come from?"

Mr. Kimall hurried to the metal cabinet where George struggled to his feet. "I finally got my side effect from the invisibility potion. Speed running!"

George coughed, clinging to the man's arm. "How'd you know to come for us?"

"You were late to the truck. I knew you'd be up to something, switching delivery days and all."

Sophie Mae rushed to Betsy, who was lying on the dirt. "Betsy?" Her bloodshot pupils turned to Sophie Mae. A small smile faded from her face.

The men hobbled toward Sophie Mae, and George knelt briefly to rub her shoulder. "There's nothing we can do for either of them. We need to leave before the security men outside come looking for the commotion."

Sophie Mae nodded but first looked in Betsy's jacket pockets. The first had nothing. The second produced two folded sheets of paper. Sophie Mae handed them to George and took Mr. Kimall's arm, stumbling toward the exit.

"Hold tight!" With a wink, Mr. Kimall shot out of the train station, both George and Sophie Mae in tow. Trash flittered along their path, but the people waiting for their train failed to notice, lost in their own thoughts.

SOPHIE MAE HELD OUT HER HANDS, AND A SMILE ETCHED across her face, lifting her rosy cheeks. Mrs. Worthington placed the black hat with a pink rose in her care. Sophie Mae curled her fingers around the soft velvet brim to keep it from sliding off her arms to the hardwood flooring.

"You've done a magnificent job," Sophie Mae said. "Does it need repair often?"

"Only when she takes to playing with Leggy in the park," Mrs. Worthington said. "She usually takes it off before it gets dirty. Thank you for delivering it, dear."

Smiling, Sophie Mae left the sewing room carrying the black hat with a carefulness usually reserved for newborn babies. Despite the rose being handcrafted from silk, it carried a fragrant scent.

Her trek down the stairs found the house as quiet as the first day she'd arrived. Back then, she had no knowledge of the invisibility potion and its ability to hide the residents' sounds. She hadn't met the rambunctious Billy, who she later learned made most of the noise. *But where are the kids, Judy and James? They love playing on the stairs.*

George rested his hands on the first-floor banister. "Where could they have gone?"

"Who are you looking for?" Sophie Mae asked.

"James and his sister. I turned for a second and they disappeared." He glanced at the giant hat in Sophie Mae's hands. "Janet is a miracle worker! The hat looks as good as new with the dirt and grass removed."

"I'm on my way to deliver it to Mary Louise. You know how she loves to wear it downtown on your walks."

"Could you watch for the kids on your way to the barn?" George asked. "I told them about their mother's passing. They didn't take it well. I wish Oscar was here. He is better at this sort of thing."

"I'll keep a lookout for them." Sophie Mae swallowed hard. "Those poor children. Losing your family is difficult and heartbreaking, especially when you're so young. Did you tell them the whole truth about Brunhold?"

"I told them what they can understand. We can fill in the details later."

SOPHIE MAE PASSED through the opened barn doors to the fifteen-square-foot shelving unit built along the far wall.

Oscar D had constructed it to organize Mary Louise's hats and accessories. The cubbies' openings were huge, and the empty one at the top was out of reach. Gently, she placed it next to a blue ribbon, knowing Mary Louise would reshelf it when she returned to the barn.

Sniffles followed by a low cry caught her ear. She scanned the interior of the barn. "Hello? Anyone here?"

A rustling came from the loft. Sophie Mae picked up a pitchfork resting against the wall. She climbed the ladder with her left hand and the last two fingers of her right. Her knee slid over the wooden edge of the loft, and she crept to the sounds coming from the corner.

It's got to be an eagle nesting. Or maybe it's a lost raccoon. Please don't be a raccoon.

Letting out a high-pitched yell, she thrust the pitchfork to the wall, hoping to scare the thing out of the barn. The creature wriggled deeper under the hay, and Sophie Mae staggered backward, tripping on Gus Grizzly's favorite wooden stool.

Her breathing quickened as she rolled into a ball, hoping to avoid being seen by the creature. Nothing happened. She uncovered her head and peeked toward the corner. James and Judy emerged from the haystack, picking bits of crunchy straw from their hair.

"What are you doing up here?" Sophie Mae asked. "This isn't a safe place for hide and seek."

James reached into his pocket and pulled out a handful of dimes and nickels. "We're counting the money Momma left in the coffee tin. We didn't want anyone to steal it."

"Why would any of us take your money?"

"I don't know, but my momma said you can't trust no one. We only have ourselves, just like she told me."

Sophie Mae looked to Judy, whose red, swollen eyes triggered tears of her own. "What did Mr. George tell you about your mother?"

James pulled Judy close. "That she was killed in the train station by a stranger. Why did she go back there? It wasn't safe for her. That's what she always said."

"Everyone here loved your mother like a sister." Sophie Mae crawled across the hay and reached out her arms. Judy's mouth hung open, and sobs poured like a stream after heavy rain. She clung to Sophie Mae, but James remained at a distance, deciding if she were the enemy.

"You've every right to be upset. Losing your parent isn't easy."

"With Momma gone, do we still have to get baths?" Judy asked.

"I'm afraid you do. You need to take baths and eat food and play outside. The last thing you should do is run away from those who love you and bring trouble on yourself."

"You're not our mother," James said wearily.

"Do you remember how we met at the train station? Judy, you were only a small baby being held by your mom. James, you were the man of the family, asking strangers for food. Your mother wouldn't want you to return to those dreadful days. If you stay here with us, you can live free and happy."

"Who will cut the crust off my sandwich?" Judy asked. "I always cut my thumb, and James never helps."

"And who will clean up the puddles of water after bath time?" James asked.

"Mr. Langston and Ms. Ruby want to help you. They'll be

like your grandparents and make sure you have everything you need. You've all had fun together so far."

Judy smiled and looked at James. "Langy is the best hide and seeker."

"Do they really want us?" James asked.

"Everyone in the house wants you. What do you say? Will you put the coins back on the shelf and stay with us?"

Pacing the hay, James rubbed his chin like Billy, stopping every five seconds to examine Sophie Mae, who stroked Judy's hair. He stopped and held out his hand. "Deal."

Shaking hands, James dropped to the hay and curled next to Sophie Mae. "Do you know any good stories?"

"I have a few good ones about Billy and his crazy pranks. Would you like to hear one?"

"Yes, please," James said, wiping his eyes. "Thank you, Miss Sophie, for taking care of us."

"You're welcome. Now on to the Adventures of Billy the Prankster."

A KNOCK AT HIS FRONT DOOR HAD ERNEST SCREECHING THE chair from the dining room table and tying his bathrobe tight around his waist. He opened the sturdy door and the woodland wreath made by Mrs. Worthington swung back and forth. He looked to the clock on the far wall. *What could George want at this early hour?*

Leaning against the door frame, he watched as George scurried about the lab, grabbing vials and boxes of herbs from the cabinet. Asking questions would be a waste of time until George came closer. Ernest's small stature came with a tiny voice.

George dropped a folded piece of paper onto the work

desk, unfamiliar to Ernest. *What has him so excited?* He raced up the stairs to the bedroom, changing into work clothes. The white lab coat coasted over the stairs as Ernest raced out the front door to the support shelf.

Swinging from the rope, he rushed to the workstation and climbed to the surface. The well-formed words written across the paper proved easy to read. *This isn't George's hand. Argan seeds? Soaked in cat urine? I hope he doesn't expect me to drink this.*

"Ah, good," George said, stumbling to the table, arms full of books. "You've found the formula. What do you think?"

"Where did you get this?" Ernest asked.

"Remember I told you about finding Betsy at the train station? Well, Sophie Mae realized Brunhold didn't have the formula, which meant Betsy still had it. We found it in her jacket pocket."

"But she stole it for him?"

"That seemed to be the plan. Maybe she had second thoughts, questioned his motives."

Ernest scanned the supplies on the table. "You think this formula will work?"

"We tested it on a plant seed, and it grew fast and big. It looked like a jungle down here. I'm sure we can tweak it a little and make it work on humans."

"Don't misunderstand my doubt, but if I end up rampaging the city as a giant head of broccoli, I'm done with magic."

THE EARLY MORNING hour became a late night in the lab. George's head lay on his crossed arms, vials and tubes pushed to the edge of the table. Snoring came from the magician as Ernest looked over the changes they'd made to the formula, searching for the mistake. Having gone over the document several times, he started fresh once again. There was always a mistake.

Mrs. Worthington tapped on the door and carried in a doll-sized cup of tea and a triangle of banana nut bread. Ernest's eyes perked open at the offering. "You're a lifesaver."

"I saw the lights from under the door. How's the growth formula coming?"

"Tedious." He sipped the warm green tea. "Can I ask you a personal question?"

"Certainly."

"George tells me your husband died from smallpox. It disrupted your life. How did you find the right path? Please don't take offense, but you seem almost better for the trauma."

Mrs. Worthington pulled up a stool. "Everyone has hardship in their lives. For me, it was losing not only the financial support of my husband but also his care and friendship. I lingered in depression for a long time after his passing.

"This home saved my family. It fed my kids and gave us a safe place to sleep. The friendships created during those first few years helped me to understand life has its trials. If we take them in stride, we can learn valuable lessons from them."

Lifting the heavy jacket from the coat rack, she draped it over George's back. Startled briefly, his hefty snoring rattled the vials lying on the desk.

Ernest bit off the last crumb of bread and paced the desktop. "I've been feeling greedy for the last few months."

"In what way?"

"When I was first shrunken, I blamed George for my troubles. My life had become a joke. I was four inches tall and living in a girl's dollhouse."

"Oh, I hope I didn't overstep my welcome, trying to make it homier for you," she said.

"I'm most grateful for what you've done, and that's part of my guilt. Since my sister Mona died, I've been on a path of vengeance. I sought to inflict pain on the world that treated us like garbage tossed to the curb. My fear turned me into a literal monster."

"Being tiny has taught me patience, the preciousness of time, and the importance of friends. When I was normal-sized, I didn't have these things. I had an empty stomach and a lousy apartment."

"Perhaps, you too, have found yourself in this estate."

"I believe you're right. Does it sound strange to say I want to stay in this small body for a little while longer and accept what it has to say about my future?"

"Not at all. It's your decision, and you are the only one who can make it. We could move your house to a better location if you like. I know George keeps strange hours."

"The sunroom at the end of the second floor would be ideal. Maybe I could start a small garden or build a pond."

"Please tell George of your decision. He's working hard to fix your situation." She gathered the cup and tray. "Let me know when you're ready to move. Perhaps we could go into town and buy you more comfortable furniture."

"Thank you, Mrs. Worthington."

"Please, call me Janet."

GEORGE'S slight whisps and snorts grew into snarls and downspouts of nasal air. Jolting awake, the coat slid off his back to the floor. His blurry vision cleared and he found Ernest pacing the top of the piled books wearing his best suit, the morning sun casting an angelic glow. George's chapped lips cracked lips he spoke. "Get your lab coat, and we'll push forward. I have a few ideas—"

"I'll pass, thank you."

George squinted at Ernest. "I must still be dreaming. If I am, can we take a stroll through the circus? I've been missing the delicious smells and excitement of the ring on a packed Friday night."

"I'm done, George," tiny Ernest said.

"With what?"

"With finding a potion to cure my height. I don't want a cure. I'm done."

George finger-brushed his hair backward. He walked to the sink and let the water run for a minute until it grew warm to the touch. Water cupped in his hands splashed to his face, and he patted the towel to his forehead.

Back at the table, he clasped his hands and smiled. "Let's start again. Good morning, Ernest. How was your night?"

"I'm still done. I finally understand I have a good life with many benefits. For one, I can travel undetected. Second, I have an entire, electrically capable house of my own."

"But I did this to you? I need to make it right."

"Nonsense. You've already made it right by welcoming me into this house and helping me to understand an eye doesn't always deserve an eye."

"Will you still help me with my experiments? You're the best for finding my mistakes. I might be wrong, but I think we're an excellent team."

"Under two conditions." Ernest buttoned his jacket. "I need smaller pencils, and I want a name."

"A name?"

"George the Great…Bruce the Loyal. I want a name."

"Oh, I see," George said, pacing the floor. "Ernest the Modest?"

"What are you implying?"

George twisted his mustache, his eyes darting about the room. "I've got it. Ernest the Revealer!"

Nodding slowly at first, he looked to George with pride. "Yes. Ernest the Revealer."

SOPHIE MAE GRIMACED at the clear sky, hoping the tame weather wouldn't give way to a severe spring storm. Ms. Catherine was returning from her charity work in Hollywood, and everything needed to be perfect.

Gus Grizzly zoomed from the barn to the field, draping a long, blue streamer between the trees. He dropped the end across a low-lying branch and returned to the barn for a green one.

"Over that branch. Yes. Now that one there," Mary Louise said, dictating the location of the streamers. "Gus, you must be more precise with your placement. Symmetry is key."

Leggy ran past the elephant carrying a string of outdoor lights in her teeth. George the Great bounced on her back, clutching her mane. Ernest huddled between her two horns, uncomfortable as he held on for life. Dropping the lights to the ground, Leggy gently cradled the last bulb on the wire with her tongue and lifted it to the air.

"Loop it around the nail, right there," George said, pointing to the wooden post supporting a basket of pansies.

Lifting her snout to the post, she waited while Ernest crawled past the tip of her moist nose to the jagged, weather-worn top. He ran laps around the nail, wrapping and securing the wire while keeping his eyes from the long drop beneath him. With a thumbs up, he crawled to the relative safety of the giraffe's horns.

"What's your plan?" Sophie Mae asked, petting the giraffe's side.

"I'm leaving that up to Leggy," George said. "She favors the zigzag layout."

Dink stumbled around the corner, her eyes barely noticeable as she struggled with a pile of white tablecloths in her arms. Ms. Ruby sashayed behind, balancing several vases of flowers like a clown act from the circus.

"Let me help," Sophie Mae said as she grabbed a few of the vases.

"Thank you, child." Ms. Ruby said. "I can't wait to see the missus. After she disappeared years ago, I can't stand letting her out of my sight."

Dink held the side of the tablecloth and thrust it high above her head, allowing it to drift to the floral etching of the table's surface. Sophie Mae brushed her hands along the starched cotton, smoothing out the air pockets. Ms. Ruby set a vase of white daisies in the middle. With the decorations mostly complete, Sophie Mae and Dink looked over the festive grounds.

"Are we ready to gather the troops?" Dink asked.

"We should, before everyone finishes their jobs and goes their own way."

Dink teetered on her tippy toes. "Meeting, everybody! Hurry!"

Leggy galloped to the girl's voice. Streamers wrapped her long neck, and a cone-shaped party hat rested on her head. George approached and handed Dink and Sophie Mae extra hats decorated with glued noodles and bits of string. He popped the elastic of his hat to his chin. "James and Judy made these for everyone."

Gus Grizzly dropped from the sky and landed next to Sophie Mae. His pupils grew large as vibrations surged through the ground. Mary Louise swaggered to the group. A nestlike hat rested on her head and was made from ostrich feathers and a big red bow. Colorful, rounded stones adorned the outer perimeter of each ear as if she were royalty.

Sophie Mae clapped as Mary Louise weaved between the residents. "You look great."

"One must do what one can."

"Has anyone seen Ernest?" Sophie Mae asked.

George cleared his voice. "Um, he went to the little boys' room."

Sophie Mae smirked and addressed the group. "Mr. Langston tells me Mr. Kimall called from the train station. He'll be here within the hour. It's time for the finishing touches."

BACK IN THE KITCHEN, Sophie Mae burned her finger on the fresh-out-of-the-oven muffin. The sweet aroma of the treat was irresistible, and she bit a chunk off the side. The secret knock, designed by Mr. Kimall and herself earlier that day, came from the door. Sophie Mae ran from the kitchen and into the foyer. "Mr. Langston. She's here."

"Thank you, Miss Sophie."

Running past the dining room table, she pushed a chair against the kitchen door and climbed on it. She spied through the round piece of glass installed by George near the top, which was finally coming in handy.

Mr. Langston opened the delivery door, and Mr. Kimall winked at the butler. "I got her here safe and sound."

"Yes," Aunt Catherine said. "Where is everyone?"

"Tending to their duties, miss. Time is nothing to waste. Might I take your bags to your room?"

"Yes, thank you."

"It's a nice day out," Mr. Kimall said. "Won't you join me for a walk through the garden?"

"As much as I love being home, I'm afraid I feel stretched thin from the trip."

"Please," he said, clutching his black cowboy hat and employing his best puppy eyes.

"You win. Perhaps a walk will do me good after sitting for so long."

Sophie Mae panicked as they started for the dining room door. Jumping from the chair, she returned it to the closest wall and cowered under the table. Spiders recoiled at her presence and crawled along their webs, hiding in the table supports.

The door swung open. Mr. Kimall's worn boots scratched across the flooring as he led Ms. Catherine's silk-and-lace dress shoes to the patio's double doors. They cleared the dining room, and Sophie Mae ran outside and around the bushes, cutting across the grass to the party. "She's coming!"

James and Judy scurried up a small tree. Ernest slid behind a vase on the first table. George, Leggy, and Mary Louise posed like Greek statues, unable to find a good hiding spot. Sophie Mae and Dink ran to the rose bushes and crouched.

"There they are," Dink said, signaling to the others.

Mr. Kimall and Ms. Catherine's voices carried with the wind. She laughed at his raccoon joke, and he complimented her dress. Turning the corner, the party came into full view.

"Surprise!" Everyone yelled, their timing out of sync.

"How wonderful!" Ms. Catherine said. "A homecoming party." As the estate residents rushed to greet her, she outstretched her arms, and kissed their cheeks. "I'm so thankful to be home. I have two bits of good news. My trip to California raised $50,000 for the people of Evenland. More importantly, a letter from Billy was delivered by the postman."

Dink sat on the soft grass. "Can you please read it?"

Ms. Catherine pulled a slim pair of reading glasses from her pocket and opened the envelope, hesitating. "Would you like to read it in private first. It might contain bad news."

"I'm sure it'll be fine," Mrs. Worthington said, joining the party late and carrying a plate of muffins. James snuck behind a bush and tracked her as she moved closer. His hand shot from the leaves, snatching one and disappearing back into the bush. She laid the plate on a table and stood next to George.

Sophie Mae stared at the letter as Aunt Catherine opened it. It crinkled like wet paper dried over a fire. A memory flooded back to her of Grandma Hattie fishing a letter from the mailbox on a rainy day, long before the droughts. She'd repositioned the wet socks hanging over the fireplace and pinned the letter to the cord, hoping it'd dry and not smudge the ink.

Sophie Mae's heart warmed as she remembered her grandma's generous eyes and soft white hair. Looking at Aunt Catherine, who prepared to read the letter aloud, the resemblance became evident.

Dear family,

I'm sorry I haven't written sooner, but it's been hectic around the camp. On the first day, they gave me a cooking job. Can you believe they let me work with knives and fire? Starting next week, I'll switch off days in the kitchen with another man and work two days a week in the forest. My first job will be clearing a path for the masonry workers building a hearth for outdoor cooking.

While I've made a few friends from my barrack, I spend most of my time with Gabe. He's a few years older than me. He's Amish, from Lancaster. While I spent my youth goofing off, he was learning to work hard and built barns. We walk into town on Sundays and discuss the differences in our upbringing.

You should get the first of my $25 paychecks in the mail soon. I wondered if you could put it away for James? When he's older,

we can use it to build him a house of
his own.
Watch out for each other. I'll be home soon.
-Billy

"Sounds like he's doing fine," George said. "Another reason to celebrate. Would you care to dance, Mrs. Worthington?"

"Yes, but please, call me Janet."

George pointed to Sophie Mae. "Music, Maestro."

Sophie Mae rushed to the portable radio on the farthest table. Dink leaned close to the speaker, shaking her head at the old orchestral pieces and waving for Sophie Mae to keep turning the dial. The red marker on the display hit a Big Band channel. Dink smiled and grabbed Sophie Mae by the hand, dragging her to the dance area under the sparkling lights.

DINK SLID INTO THE DRIVER'S SEAT OF THE ESTATE'S NEW Hillman Fourteen. Purchased for anyone in the house to use, its primary purpose was to help with charity work. Dink squeezed the giant steering wheel and turned to Ms. Catherine. "Are you sure I should drive? I don't have much experience."

"Nonsense. Mr. Kimall says you are a great driver. Very cautious and courteous. Besides, I've never driven an automobile. A horse and carriage are more my style."

Pushing the gas pedal, the car started down the gravel driveway of the estate. The car rode smoother than Mr. Kimall's old truck and lacked the massive stick shift that made the middle of the bench seat uncomfortable. Her confidence grew the farther they traveled.

Stopping outside the gate, her hands trembled at the traffic whizzing past the bumper of the car. Ms. Catherine touched her forearm. "Do you like the new automobile? Mr. Kimall helped me pick it out. It delighted the man at the shop to make the sale."

Dink found a break in the traffic and shot into the street. "It's great, but less exciting than riding Leggy into town."

"I've never had the privilege of riding a giraffe," Ms. Catherine said. "I heard from George you were a big help while I was gone. You even sat in the city council meetings."

"Someone had to figure out the next round of city ordinances. Everyone else in the house had a job, and I wanted to help. Now I've seen what's going on there, I think attending the meetings should be mandatory. Some of those guys are only out for money."

"I was hoping you'd say as much. Would you mind more responsibility for the charity? I received my cut of the donations in the mail from the Hollywood tour, and it's enough to build a decent number of houses for the families in the Hooverville."

"Really?" Dink said, surprised. "That's great. They all need a clean place to live. When will the construction begin? How many houses?"

"That all depends on you, my dear."

Dink stopped at the red light and turned to Ms. Catherine. "What do you mean?"

"I'm putting you in charge of the project."

"You can't. I know nothing about building homes, and those people need shelter."

"Your familiarity with the local politicians should aid you in getting favorable deals on land and securing the needed permits to build. I've asked another to assist you with purchasing building supplies and the overall architecture of the homes. You might know him, he's a local boy. Thomas Clarkson."

"Thomas? *The Thomas* who works at the hardware store?"

"I suppose. Mr. Clarkson's father owns the hardware store and the lumberyard here in town. At the moment, Thomas is working for the government WAP program, and is gaining a wealth of experience constructing government buildings. I've secured his services, plus a small team of workers to build the homes." Ms. Catherine looked out the window. "Oh, this is the place."

The Hillman slid to the curb, and Dink killed the engine. Ms. Catherine stepped to the sidewalk, and Dink followed, looking at the sign above the door.

Evenland Hardware
Family owned since 1886

"What are we doing here?"

"We have a meeting with the elder Mr. Clarkson, so we might introduce the two of you and begin the necessary paperwork. Time waits for no man."

Ms. Catherine nodded to passers-by on the street as Dink opened the door.

"Good afternoon," the cashier said. "Mr. Clarkson is awaiting your arrival. Straight back and to the right, ma'am."

"Thank you."

Ms. Catherine walked down the long aisle to the back of

the store, stopping to look over the products displayed on the end caps. Turning to Dink, she held a tool that looked more like a giant necklace. "What do you suppose this does?" Catherine asked with a curious tone.

Dink shrugged, not caring to guess, her mind preoccupied with the idea of Thomas being in the store. Eventually, she'd have to talk to him. The feeling of snakes coiling in her gut made her lightheaded.

"It's called a plumb bob," Thomas said, taking the cone-shaped brass object by its string. "It helps when framing basement walls."

"What did I tell you!" Ms. Catherine said. "He knows his stuff."

"Please, come into the office. My dad has been talking about our joint venture."

Dink's eyelids failed to blink.

"You can come too, Lillian," Thomas said. "I heard we are going to be working together on the new housing development. It should be a blast."

"Yeah, a blast." Dink squirmed. "The problem is, I don't know how to build a house."

"And I don't understand Evenland's political structure. That'll prove more valuable than framing a wall. Ms. Gardenia has told me you're friendly with a few of the bigwig politicians."

"I wouldn't say friends. They know I live with Ms. Catherine, and she's the richest woman in the city."

"And they *will* want to support the richest woman in town, I'm sure." He started toward the office. "We're gonna have to spend a lot of time together looking over designs and land maps."

"Yes, I guess we will."

"I'll teach you the tricks of construction if you explain politics to me."

"Alright," Dink said. "But don't expect too much. I'm only learning myself."

"And maybe driving. I put off learning so I could work and save for my own wagon." He met her eyes. "How did you learn? Few women drive cars, much less teenagers."

"Mr. Kimall taught me in his work truck. He makes deliveries for the estate. And I'll have you know I'm a very cautious and courteous driver."

"I didn't mean any offense, just curious. So, can you teach me? It'll come in handy when we start to build. Running supplies takes lots of trucks."

Dink nodded, feeling the heat from her blushing cheeks.

They entered the office well-suited for two people, but with the elder Mr. Clarkson, Thomas, Dink, and Ms. Catherine, it was downright tiny. The two youths leaned against the wall as Ms. Catherine and Mr. Clarkson hammered out their alliance's finer details.

Thomas leaned to Dink and whispered, "Maybe we can have our meetings at the estate? You can show me around. I've always wanted to see what's behind the giant gate."

"That would be—" Dink froze once again, this time because of Mary Louise. *He'll see her talking, and the potion will be found out. No, I can tell her to stay quiet. That might work...maybe?*

"Is that a bad idea? We can have them somewhere else."

"No, it's fine," she whispered, not confident in her answer.

Sitting next to the bed, Sophie Mae slid the one-foot-square box from underneath. Flecks of the white paint fell to the floor, unveiling more of the stained wooden surface. She pinched the flower-shaped latch in her fingers and thought of Myrt, the box's previous owner.

Oscar D had given the seed storage box to Sophie Mae after Myrt's funeral. Not needing to keep seed for the next season, Sophie Mae used it as storage for her most personal items. Inside, she kept the letter from the retired traveling box, the fake will of Aunt Catherine, and the train ticket, which reminded her that life was about more than food and shelter.

A pressed flower from Myrt's funeral sat on the bottom,

surrounded by a handful of buttons given to her by older ladies in the community. From behind a red petal peeked the gold ring given to her by Mrs. Baker from the Hooverville. She picked it up and looked at an engraving showing it once belonged to Betsy.

Trying the ring on for size, she found it fit just right. *What should I do with this? Donate it to the church for supplies or give it to James?*

Sliding the gold ring into her pocket, she returned the box to the bed and headed for the door. A single step into the hallway and she fell into the wall as James ran past wearing a towel cape. A stick dropping bits of bark on the wooden floor waved in the air. "You'll never escape justice!"

Watching the boy sprint down the hallway made her think better of giving it to him, at least when he was so young.

Climbing the stairs to the third floor, Sophie Mae knocked on her Aunt Catherine's door and waited. Ms. Ruby answered and smiled. "Miss Sophie, please come in. The missus is resting, but I know she'd love to see you."

"Thank you."

"I'll leave you two alone. I feel *justice* is calling from the hall."

Sophie Mae walked to Aunt Catherine's bed, layered in blue-tinted light streaming from the windows. "Sophie Mae. Come here, my dear. Tell me, how does your ankle feel? I've noticed you limping."

"It's fine. Better than it has been."

"Pull up a chair, young lady. What's on your mind?"

Sophie Mae lifted the wooden chair from the vanity and put it within arm's reach of Aunt Catherine. She sat down and handed her the gold ring.

"My, has it happened already? How exciting! Who's the lucky beau?"

"It's not mine," Sophie Mae blushed. "It belonged to Betsy. Mrs. Baker gave it to me for safe keeping. What should I do with it now Betsy's gone?"

"Betsy lived a hard life, like most people these days," she handed the ring back to Sophie Mae. "We have several options. We could sell it and give the money to the community or simply give it back to Mrs. Baker. Maybe Betsy wanted her to have it all along."

"You might be right."

"But my heart tells me to keep it safe for little James and Judy. It's the only thing their mother left behind."

"Isn't it wrong to keep it until they're older?" Sophie Mae asked. "I mean it belongs to them, and they might resent us for not telling them sooner."

"Either way poses a risk. I'll let you decide."

Sophie Mae paced the room. Looking to the glass ceiling, she remembered floating with Billy. At that moment, she understood the room was essential to Billy's memory, just as the ring will be necessary to James and Judy.

"We need to save it for them. James will probably use it as a treasure in a pirate game if we give it to him now."

"Smart decision," Aunt Catherine said. "You can store it in the safe."

A painting of a grand forest hung on the brick wall of the room. The last time she'd been in the master suite, it was wintertime and snow covered the tops of the acrylic trees. Now, red and yellow flowers dotted the landscape as spring had arrived. Squirrels ran past, searching for the perfect place to bury nuts for the future. *I might never get used to the magic Mr. George puts on these pictures.*

Swinging the framed painting open like a door, she found the safe built into the wall. Sophie Mae turned the small knob on the front to the numbers entrusted to her by Catherine not long after losing her childhood memories to the traveling box. The door clicked, and she drew it open.

Bonds from the Great War were stacked next to the single gold bar kept for emergencies. A folded piece of lace hid the chain of a gold necklace. Sophie Mae placed the ring inside and picked up the heart-shaped locket she'd put there years ago. She opened the heart and smiled at her Grandma Hattie's face. Her joyful expression faded as she retreated into a forgotten memory.

The smell of dirt and pollen filled the air as she stared at the porch of the Drycrop farm. Rocking chairs lined the deck, their shape distorted by the dozens of layers of paint coating the surface. Grandma Hattie rocked in the seat knitting a sweater and talking to the elderly neighbor in the chair next to her.

Bless her heart was said more than once as Sophie Mae walked from the gate to the women. The neighbor turned to Sophie Mae. "It's about time you showed up. Your grandma was worried sick."

"Now, don't be too hard on the girl," Grandma Hattie said. "She got here as soon as she could."

"What's going on?" Sophie Mae asked.

"Why, can't you see I'm knitting you a sweater?"

"But it's so hot outside?"

Grandma Hattie dropped the soft yarn to her lap. "Be prepared for anything that comes your way, dear child." The women laughed as Sophie Mae was pulled back into the Gardenia Estate's blue bedroom.

"Bless your heart," Aunt Catherine said.

"What?"

"Well, you look like you lost your dog. Take the necklace. It's yours, remember?"

"I think I do. Strangely enough, I think I do."

Enjoying the Journey?

Please consider leaving a review at Amazon.
A line or two of your thoughts would
be much appreciated.

Thanks!

As a free-range child Mason Bell spent most summers and weekends outside climbing trees and jumping fences.

All that energy came from the sweet neighborhood grandmas who offered thick slices of cake for a bit of conversation. Each had their own version of life back in the day.

These stories, combined with the freedom to roam, spurred Mason's creativity and storytelling.

Mason Bell lives in South Texas with her husband and two cats, Frodo and Fat Hobbit.

Sign up for the Newsletter
www.MasonBellAuthor.com

facebook.com/MasonBellAuthor
instagram.com/MasonBellAuthor

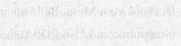

ALSO BY MASON BELL

The Most Magical Beginning

The Most Spectacular Traveling Box

An imprint of Two Turkey Publishing, LLC
4501 Magnolia Cove Dr. Ste 201, Kingwood, Texas 77345

Names: Bell, Mason, 1975-

Title: The most perilous sideshow : a Sophie Mae adventure / Mason Bell.

Description: Kingwood, Texas: Two Turkey Publishing, LLC, [2020] | Series: A Sophie Mae adventure.

| Audience: middle-grade.

Identifiers: ISBN: 978-1-7359072-7-7 (hardcover) |978-1-7359072-3-9 (paperback) | 978-1-7359072-4-6 (ebook) | 978-1-7359072-5-3 (Kindle) | LCCN: 2020922945)

Subjects: LCSH: Orphans--Oklahoma--Juvenile fiction. | Dust Bowl Era, 1931-1939--Juvenile fiction. | Magic--Juvenile fiction. | Magicians--Juvenile fiction. | Elephants--Juvenile fiction. | Manors-- Minnesota--Juvenile fiction. | Sideshows--Juvenile fiction. | Strangers--Juvenile fiction. | Danger perception--Juvenile fiction. | CYAC: Orphans--Oklahoma--Fiction. | Dust Bowl Era, 1931-1939--Fiction. | Magic--Fiction. | Magicians--Fiction. | Elephants--Fiction. | Dwellings-- Minnesota--Fiction. | Sideshows--Fiction. | Strangers--Fiction. | Danger--Fiction. | LCGFT: Adventure stories. | Historical fiction. | Children's .

Classification: LCC: PZ7.1.B45232 M68 202 | DDC: [Fic]--dc23

CPSIA information can be obtained
at www.ICGtesting.com
Printed in the USA
LVHW041917270821
696291LV00022B/2397